*All of the historical research, mythology
and geographical locations in this book are real.*

PROLOGUE

Ireland, 32 years ago

The pale-skinned woman stood on the edge of the cliff, looking out at the dark ocean, as she often did when the moon was bright and the wind still. Her toes gripped the tufts of grass that pushed up through the rocky soil. A crisp winter breeze stroked her long charcoal hair and tugged playfully at the hem of her white cotton dress. The indigo blue waves undulated below, stretching the shimmering reflection of the full moon towards the horizon, and foaming as they crashed against the rocks. Her awareness fixed firmly in the deep waters below her, she almost didn't hear the approaching footsteps; two sets—one of a heavyset man, one of a young boy. By the time she turned to greet them, the dagger was sticking out of her abdomen. The handle was polished white glass that shone like abalone, and twisted around the center. A shearing pain spread through her torso, causing her to stumble. Blood soaked into her dress and dripped down her leg. Her first thought was how difficult it was going to be to get the stain out. But then she realized, she was never going home.

"Sorry about this, love. But we can't have your kind walking around up here. I've allowed it long enough," the man said. His tone was apologetic, but he didn't look sorry at all. There was a smug enthusiasm in his eyes that told her he'd been looking forward to this moment. His companion was just a child, with a face that looked both terrified and determined. His unruly hair was bright orange, even in the darkness.

"Don't do this," the woman said, gasping for breath. "You can't imagine the consequences it will bring."

"Ready?" the man said, ignoring her. The boy nodded, holding out a silver flask, etched with symbols.

With a sudden jerk, the man tore the knife from the woman's body, while the boy caught the spurt of blood in the container. The flask began to glow as it filled. The woman shuddered, but then her eyes filled with a smoky blackness, until even the whites of her eyes were black.

"There you are," the man teased. "I was hoping you'd reveal your true self. Any last words? I would offer to bring a message to your daughter, but she'll be joining you soon enough."

"You've just destroyed the human race," the woman said, in a gravelly, unearthly voice. "And sealed your own fate."

Faster than he could follow, the woman grabbed the knife from his hands and plunged it deep into his shoulder. He screamed in agony. The woman's arm shot out at lightning speed with supernatural power, punching through the man's chest. Her bloody hand jutted through the other side. Blood gurgled from his mouth and his eyes widened in pain. "Take care of the girl!" he shouted to the boy with his last breath. Then the bloody pair tumbled off the edge of the cliff as one, plunging like a red comet towards the dark water, and were lost into the crashing waves below.

1

Present Day

I've always believed that the world was full of magic. Maybe not the spells and wands kind of magic, but at least the subtle, intuitive kind—like that TV show I watched about a woman who sensed her mother was dying from thousands of miles away, and got there in time to say goodbye. But when my dad's silver Acura smashed through the guardrail on highway 99, sending both my parents tumbling down the side of a ravine and killing them both, I didn't feel a thing. I was warming up backstage in the auditorium of Arcadia High School, devising new forms of torture for Timmy Grant, who was flirting with Emily Peters just two weeks after he kissed me behind the props closet. And I was also pissed off at my parents for not being on time to my performance.

"I'm sure they'll be here any minute," Beth said, trying to console me.

"It's fine," I lied. "I'm fine." It was generous of Beth, my best friend since third grade, to assume I was worried about my parents, rather than how Timmy was leaning in really close to Emily now and touching her cheek, in front of everybody, and my heart was ripping in half because I really thought he liked me. (What gave me that impression, you ask? Maybe it was because he said, while looking into my eyes and touching my cheek, "I really like you.")

"He's a douchebag," Beth said, following my gaze and finally clueing in.

"Whatever," I said with a shrug, forcibly removing the big sad puppy dog eyes from my face that I was secretly hoping he'd notice. I replaced them with a calm determination that felt more natural. "I'm so over it." Life goes on. *Que sera sera.* I'll just ignore the pain, win some scholarships and go off to college, where I'll meet a dashing prince. Or something like that.

Okay, now I was getting a little worried about my parents: the concert had already started and I was going on stage soon. *It's only the biggest concert performance of the year.* So my parents are late. It happens. But in all my fifteen years, I don't think my mom had ever been late, for anything, which probably explained the dark terror that was creeping under my skin and sinking deep into my bones. I have an overactive imagination, my teachers have said, and I use it to dwell on horrible things. When I was little I had separation anxiety and I'd draw all the awful things that could be happening to my mom after she dropped me off at preschool. They even thought about making me see a shrink, suspecting I was either a twisted psychopath (and a very dangerous three-year-old, like those ones in the horror movies) or that I had some hidden childhood trauma. Neither of which was true. My mother explained this to my teachers (which means: she stood up and shouted in their faces, pumping her fist, and even throwing desks around, the way my dad tells the story). But she learned not to make me wait, and to always be there for me when I was expecting her. Punctuality had always been my comfort blanket. *Until tonight.*

My stomach was in knots and I clenched my fists in frustration. Mom had circled the date in red ink on the calendar months ago—and there were supposed to be representatives from prestigious universities in the audience tonight seeking out fresh talent to lavish scholarships upon. And I had a solo.

I couldn't think of any justifiable excuse for them not to be in their front row seats an hour early. I poked my head from the side of the curtain as the orchestra warmed up. I could see the two seats I'd saved, the red ribbon I'd wrapped around them taunting me with a sly gleam. I was angry, but behind the anger, scorpions of anxiety were clawing through my stomach. I knew it was probably something simple and stupid, like traffic on 101, and that worrying right now was wasted energy. I needed to stay calm so I'd nail all the right notes and not forget the fancy Italian words to my solo.

In quali eccessi, o Numi... in quai misfatti orribili, tremendi, I hummed to myself, reciting the words in my head. But then I made the mistake of translating the words into English, and the weight of the augurous passage filled my heart with unwarranted despair.

In what excesses, O Heavens, In what horrible, terrible crimes...

We weren't doing the full Don Giovanni, just a few musical scores, but my solo was one of the highlights of the performance. I was the star of the high school production—and as a sophomore, no less. It was really quite an accomplishment, or so my mother had been telling me all week.

Where the hell are they?

When they introduced me, Clara Clark, I stepped as boldly as I dared onto the stage in my blue Disney princess dress with puffy sleeves—the closest the drama department had to an 18th-century opera star outfit. I blinked against the bright spotlights, nodded at the conductor to let him know I was ready, and began to sing on cue. I was halfway through my piece when my eyes adjusted enough to make out the audience. I tried to ignore the two empty seats in front, but that damned red ribbon kept drawing my eye.

I closed my eyes and let myself melt into the music. My fears and worries abated, and the warm, full notes bubbled up from my diaphragm like honey. I could feel them soaring over the crowd like sparrows. Then I started to connect with the audience. I felt my voice pique their full attention, almost like it grabbed their chin and forced them to look up at me. I watched them put away their cell phones and stop reading the program. I felt their hearts begin to race, in sync with mine, as the music built towards the crescendo. All their private thoughts were washed away by the river of my singing, and my emotions became their emotions. At least that's how I liked to imagine it. Maybe it was just a little game I was playing with myself. Maybe it wasn't real.

But then my eyes were open again, and there was movement in the back of the auditorium, and the game was spoiled. Two uniformed police officers were talking with the music director, and he gestured to the stage. *To me.* When the three of them stopped talking and looked at me with sad eyes, it felt like someone had punched me in the stomach. Because then I knew. And I knew it wasn't like it was in kindergarten, when I'd cry and then my mom would sweep in and show me that all of my fears were misplaced, and that she'd always been there for me. I knew this time it was real, and no one was coming to comfort me. My eyes brimmed with tears, but I forced myself to finish the song. Somehow my brain could sing in Italian while another voice in my head was screaming.

2

The days following the accident were a blur of gray suits and black dresses, white flowers on polished mahogany caskets, hushed conversations and furtive glances in my direction. The funeral was torture. I have a dark sense of humor that few people get, and a passive-aggressive sarcasm that comes from having an overbearing mother and a fear of any kind of conflict. At school those attributes just made me weird and quirky. At funerals however, I soon found out, dealing with the death of my parents through sarcasm and lame jokes wasn't a socially acceptable way to express my grief. So I stuffed my face with cheese and crackers until I couldn't do anything more than nod and mumble "thank you" when people offered me their condolences.

After the concert, I went home with Beth's family. I was excused from school for the time being, and Beth's father had helped arrange the funeral. Like I said, those days are kind of blurry. It wasn't until Beth's dad drove me to the appointment with the state of Arizona that life snapped back into focus.

I was wearing my blue Doc Martens, black skinny jeans and a baggy T-shirt. After the concert that destroyed my life, I'd retrieved the red ribbon and now wore it around my wrist like a bracelet. It reminded me of what I'd lost. I felt shame and guilt thinking that I spent the last moments of my parents' lives angry at them. The ribbon was like my own personal scarlet letter.

"You said before, you don't have any other relatives, is that right, hon?" the social worker asked me. I think she said her name was Janet or Janice. She chewed on her pen and peered at me over her faux-vintage horn rimmed glasses.

I shook my head. "My dad's parents died when I was young."

"And your mom—"

"Left England when she was sixteen," I said. The subtle edge in my voice shouted, *I've already answered this question a hundred times!* The office decor was trying too hard to be cheerful, with yellow wallpaper and colorful posters. They were encroaching on my sensitive vision, and I'd been sitting in this chair for at least ten minutes. I bounced my knees in frustration.

Janet or Janice put on a confused face—not actual confusion: a parody of what a confused face is supposed to look like—and ruffled her papers. I hate it when people do that. The face thing, not the ruffling. "Hmmm...Our records show your mother was from Ireland," the woman continued. "See here?" She gestured at a photocopy of my mom's passport and green card. "Last name, Daly."

I grabbed the papers from her and narrowed my eyes. The photograph in the documents was clearly my mother. Large dark eyes, silky black hair, the smooth, porcelain skin I'd always admired. But the name was wrong.

"This is a mistake," I said. "My mother's maiden name was Bishop, before she met my dad and became Branna Clark."

"I understand that's what you've been told." The woman adjusted her glasses. "Maybe your mother just wanted to try out a new name, for fun, when she got to America?"

"That's impossible," I said. I knew my mother. Fun wasn't something she did spontaneously. *What the hell is going on?*

"Anyhow, we've gotten in touch with her biological father, Aedan Daly, in Northern Ireland, and he's confirmed that he's her father, your grandfather. Since you're only fifteen, he's your legal guardian. He's made arrangements for you to go and live with him."

My jaw dropped open and my heart skipped a beat. A few seconds later I remembered to take a breath. *I have a grandfather?* I stood up, but my shaking legs betrayed me, and I sank back into the chair again.

Beth's father, who'd come with me, leaned forward and said, "Listen, I think it would be better for her to stay with us, at least until she finishes high school. After the death of her parents, moving to a new school—a new *country*, just seems like too much."

I didn't like that they were talking about me like I wasn't there. But I was also glad Mr. Reed had come with me. My heart filled with hope: surely they would let me stay with Beth's family instead of moving to live with some stranger in another country.

"I understand this is a huge adjustment, especially after the accident—"

The hope died in my chest, and panic consumed me. In desperation, I stood up and started shouting—which for me, means speaking quietly in a scathing voice.

"It wasn't an accident," I said, seething. "It was some stupid asshole, probably drunk, who murdered my parents." Actually the police hadn't mentioned another driver. But what else could have happened? The police said they hadn't found anything wrong with the car, and my dad was an excellent driver. Cars don't just spin out of control for no reason.

The woman closed the folder and gave Mr. Reed a look that said *there's nothing we can do.*

I raised my voice a little. "What about school? My house? All my friends... my *whole life* is here." Definitely not an indoor voice.

"Ireland has excellent schools, and I know you don't want to hear this right now, but you'll make new friends," she said, with a saccharine smile I wanted to slap off her face.

"I can't just move to Ireland," I said. I crossed my arms and stood in a way that suggested they would have to crate me up and ship me there against my will.

"Unfortunately, there's very little we can do legally. If you had no living relatives at all, the court would have to make a decision, and you'd probably be moved to a foster home; in which case living with Beth's family might be a possibility. But we've had a lot of experience in these matters and it's almost always best if a relative is available. Honestly, it's much better this way. Plus, there's the matter of your parents' will."

That shut me up. I took a deep breath and swallowed loudly.

"The will?" I asked.

"Your mother named her father as your godparent and legal guardian, in case anything ever happened to both your parents."

Damn. Here I was thinking the state was trying to pull a fast one; they'd made some clerical error, and the corporate bureaucracy was going to send me off to live with a complete stranger: my mom would be furious. *Bungling imbeciles*, she'd call them to their faces. If she were here. But a will, mentioning this Aedan Daly?

"You're saying… she lied to me my whole life and never even mentioned I have an Irish grandfather, but she left me to him in a will like a piece of furniture?"

"I agree the circumstances are unusual, but I'm sure she had a reasonable explanation—"

"But what if he's a psycho?" I asked. My brow prickled with sweat and my skin felt hot and sticky. The stuffy air made it hard to breathe.

"Your parents had the right to appoint a legal guardian without a formal court appointment, but we'd never put you at risk. We've contacted the local authorities to check his records and get character witnesses, and everyone says he's a perfectly lovely man. Maybe your mother had a falling out with him but always hoped you'd get to meet him—that would explain the will."

"What about college?" I interrupted.

"You'll still have your American citizenship of course, so you can apply to schools here, although Europe has excellent universities as well, so you may discover you change your mind. And after the house is sold—"

"You're selling my *house*?" This was too much. It felt like my whole world was dissolving around me. My knuckles went white as I clung to the back of my chair; a single point of certainty in a spiraling universe.

"The property assets will be liquidated and go into a trust fund for you. That, together with the life insurance policies, should be more than enough to cover the tuition for wherever you go to school, and then some. It's all laid out very clearly in the will. Your parents certainly had their affairs in order."

No surprise there, my mother always thought a thousand moves ahead. I put my face in my hands and took several deep breaths. Then I opened my mouth again to argue, but nothing came out. I was out of objections, and Janet—Janice or whatever her name was knew it. She patted me on the shoulder, then gathered up all the paperwork into a folder.

"When do I have to leave?" I slumped down in my seat.

***

A week later I was on an airplane leaving behind everything I'd ever known, to live with a man I'd never met. And I was heading to a town I couldn't even pronounce: *Portballintrae*. My parents' deaths brought out one surprise after another. And not a surprise like a puppy in a box under the Christmas tree.

At the airport, I kept imagining a stay of execution: this was a huge mistake, and somebody was going to come running through the terminal shouting to stop the plane. They'd messed up the paperwork. It was all just a misunderstanding. I thought it would be like one of those romantic movies. But no one came to save me.

"Everything is going to be fine, Clara," Beth said, giving me a tight hug. "We'll keep in touch. I'll come visit you next summer." I nodded, and tried to smile. So far I'd put on a brave face and been polite to everyone, but I was too tired to keep up the act. When I'd gone through security, I turned back one last time to wave goodbye.

"No Beth, it won't," I said under my breath.

When the plane took off, I felt more alone than I'd ever felt in my life. Apart from Beth and her parents, no one would even miss me. I had no expectations, nor hope for my future. Just a calm, deep sorrow, and a numbness that covered my body like a blanket of ash. A few days after the accident, the police had dropped off the personal items my parents had on them at the time of their deaths. I'd taken my mother's iPhone, both because it was a newer model than mine, and because I couldn't bear to leave it behind. Now I scrolled through all of her favorite music, listening to each song one by one.

I transferred planes at JFK, had some barely acceptable Chinese food, and headed to the next gate. By the time I boarded the plane and found my seat, I couldn't keep my eyes open. I fell asleep before the plane took off. When I woke up and glanced out the window, all I could see was the sun on the horizon, reflecting over the expansive body of water below. It dawned on me that I'd never seen the ocean from above before, apart from movies and TV. Arizona was one of the driest states in the U.S., and on family holidays we went to places like Yellowstone. I remembered a camping trip, where my dad taught me how to build a fire, and we roasted marshmallows and sang silly songs. My mother cooked baked beans and hotdogs, and it was the best thing I'd ever tasted.

Thinking about my family on vacation brought out the tears. For the past week I'd shut them out by keeping busy. (By "busy" I mean glued to my iPhone, checking every few minutes for more sympathy comments on my Facebook wall, feeling a thrill when Timmy Grant posted, *"you're moving? That sucks,"* and congratulating myself when I refused to hit *like* or comment a reply.) But now, stuck in a tiny seat with no leg room or cell phone signal for a ten-hour flight, I was trapped with my emotions, and I couldn't hold them in anymore.

The sudden loss of my parents was bad enough, but the shock and confusion I felt after the revelation of my mother's secrets was too much to handle. Every time I let myself think about it, my thoughts spiraled out of control. *Why would my mom lie to me about where she was from?* I'd always thought of myself as being a little bit English. I even had a poster of Big Ben and double-decker buses in my bedroom. I felt like an idiot now. I didn't even know who I was anymore.

Did my dad know who she really was? And why hadn't she told me about my grandfather? What was she running from? Why had she left home as a teenager—what if this Aedan Daly *was* a monster? How could the State of Arizona just ship me off to live with someone I'd never even met?

My parents were dead, life as I knew it was over, and *nobody* cared. Sure people were talking about it right now, but in a few weeks most of the kids at my high school wouldn't be able to remember my name—although that's not saying much. To be honest, there probably weren't that many who knew my name anyway.

I gave in to my self-pity and sobbed for at least an hour. Part of me felt bad for the guy sitting next to me, shifting uncomfortably and trying in vain to read a spy novel; from the cover, something with explosions and gunfights and snowmobiles. The stewardess stopped by more than once to see if there was anything she could get me, but I just waved her off and said I was fine. Finally I was out of tears and my body shut down into an exhausted sleep.

I woke up hours later and watched the sun glinting off the blue vastness below for a long time. It was hypnotic, and somehow calming. They brought around the breakfast cart, with a ham croissant and some coffee, and we landed about an hour later at the Dublin International Airport. I collected my things, splashed water on my face in the restroom, and followed the line of people from the airplane.

I went through customs, and then waited at the luggage carousel for my suitcases. They'd given me a few hours to decide which of my possessions I loved enough to keep. "Don't worry about it too much," the estate manager had told me. "Anything you forget to bring, I'm sure you can just buy a new one when you get to Ireland." My suitcases were mostly full of books and sentimental keepsakes. The largest item was the vintage Remington Noiseless typewriter my dad bought for me when I was nine. We found it in a second-hand shop, and he spent days fixing the keys so they wouldn't stick together. I think he was excited about the idea of me becoming a writer.

I spent months typing things, eating up stacks of pristine white paper, starting dozens of stories, but by the time I was eleven I was more into singing instead. For years it was just an expensive paperweight and decoration. But then I started to feel guilty for not using it, and I imagined the silence emitting from my room was heavy and meaningful. So I began to spend a little time each day just hitting the keys. I didn't put any paper in it, I just typed my thoughts and let them disappear into the air. It became a therapy of sorts. I fed my secret fears, hopes and regrets into that typewriter, and it absolved my confessions with the satisfying clicks of the metal keys. Despite its name, it wasn't completely noiseless, and I adored the subtle give of the keys against the persistent force of my downward stroke. Leaving it behind would have felt like leaving a part of myself.

I heaved my bags onto a luggage cart and pushed it out past the *Nothing to Declare* sign, into the arrivals terminal, and glanced around. It didn't take long to find my grandfather—he had a big sign with my name on it and was waving at me. I would have recognized him anyway, from the photo I'd been given of an old man in a plaid scarf. "Welcome to Ireland, Clara!" my grandfather greeted me as I rolled up to him. I pulled the edges of my lips up in what I hoped passed for a smile. He gathered me into a tight hug, patting my hair awkwardly.

"Hi," I said, pulling away.

He wasn't as old as I would have guessed from the picture. Late 50s, maybe, but tall and fit, with dark hair tinged with gray, and blue eyes that sparkled when he smiled. He looked friendly enough... but looks could be deceiving.

"You can call me Aedan," he said. "Or Grandpa of course, once we get more familiar with each other. I'm so sorry for your loss. What happened to Branna—" his face twisted into a pained expression, and I remembered he'd just lost his daughter. *Maybe I wasn't all alone in this.*

"I mean, both your parents, of course," he caught himself, "though I never had the pleasure of meeting your father. I can't imagine how hard all this must be for you." He handed me a white rose, a simple but touching gesture that made my eyes water. I brought it up to my nose and inhaled to show my appreciation.

"Thanks," I said, with another little smile, but then I stopped, feeling self-conscious.

How long after the death of one's parents was smiling illicit?

He grabbed the cart and pointed the way to the parking lot. As he loaded my suitcases into his old blue jeep, he asked how my flight was, whether I'd eaten on the plane, and if I was jet-lagged. I climbed in next to him and buckled up. Then we drove out of the airport and onto the highway heading north.

The silence was heavy enough to notice, and I started thinking of topics to broach. But I could only think of smart remarks or cutting bits of sarcasm. I didn't trust myself not to have a meltdown or blurt out something I'd regret, so I just bit my lip until he finally broke the silence.

"I hope it's okay, I've enrolled you for school already at Ballymoney High. The principal said it would be better to get you started as soon as possible, so you don't fall too far behind everyone else as the semester goes on. You're scheduled to start on Monday. But if that's too soon..." he drifted off, glancing sideways to check my reaction.

It was Friday, so I'd have all weekend to settle in. I shrugged, "It's fine, I guess. Do I need to... prepare anything?" He looked relieved to discuss such trivial topics. I wanted to grab him and shout, *why did my mother leave? Why did she lie to me about it?*

But I kept my emotions in check. I needed to wait this out and see what happened.

"I thought we'd go shopping tomorrow, so I can show you around town, and buy some supplies and things. You don't have to worry about clothes, because all the kids wear uniforms here, but you may want to pick up any – err – toiletries and such, feminine products…" he coughed but continued bravely.

"Tomorrow night I've organized a Wake at the pub my mate Liam owns, for your parents—or mostly your mother. A lot of folks in town remember her and want to pay their respects. Liam's son Derry is two years older than you, but there's another lass in your year that lives near me, I've asked her to come by and help get you ready for school."

"That sounds… nice," I conceded. For the first time, I realized my mother grew up here. People knew her. She must have had friends. People she was close to. Maybe someone would be able to tell me why she left. If she and Aedan did have a falling out, he probably wasn't the right person to ask.

Suddenly my brain kicked in, reacting to something Aedan said. *Uniforms.* Like, the short skirt and sweater vest and everything? I groaned inwardly. I was already dreading being the awkward new student. Now I wouldn't even have the security of my comfy jeans and a hoodie I could disappear into.

As we left the city, buildings thinned out and were replaced by rolling green hills and ancient stone walls. We even passed the ruins of an old church. When we had to stop for a flock of sheep I almost laughed out loud, it was so stereotypically Ireland. I had the impulse to pull out my mom's iPhone and snap selfies with the sheep behind me, but I resisted. It seemed self-indulgent, and really American. I'm not sure why I cared what Aedan thought of me, but I might be stuck living with him for a while, and I didn't want to make the wrong first impression. I didn't get cell service here anyway.

I took a few deep breaths and leaned back in my seat. *I'm in Ireland*, I told myself, trying to make it seem real. Even though I was grieving, and my mind constantly gnawed at my situation in worry, part of me felt... excited. It was the first time since the accident that I felt even a glimmer of happiness.

Maybe Beth was right. Maybe, somehow, everything really was going to be okay. But then I caught myself, and my pessimism asserted itself. *No it isn't. Nothing's ever going to be alright, ever again.*

3

I slept in the next morning but the smell of strong coffee roused me. Miscreant, Aedan's longhair grey cat, hissed at me from the green easy chair in the living room. We were briefly introduced the night before—he scratched my arm and then ran out of the room.

"Morning to you too," I said.

Aedan left out a simple breakfast—a few slices of thick, hearty brown bread, fresh butter and homemade jam. Everything else in the past two weeks had tasted like cardboard. I don't know if the change of scenery had refreshed my taste buds or if the food was actually better here, but I ate everything. It was deceptively simple fare, but I marveled at the tastes and textures. The kitchen smelled like lavender, cheese and cedar. There was a note on the table.

At work all day, sorry to leave you alone—I left a present for you outside if you want to explore the town a little. Tonight we'll head over to the pub at 8 for some dinner and company.

Next to the note was a tourist brochure that looked at least ten years old. It told me Portballintrae had about 700 inhabitants, and that "the charming village also boasts a sheltered harbor, a quiet beach, a plethora of interesting rock pools and a beautifully situated nine-hole golf course." *Great. Just what I need, a bunch of rich tourists swinging clubs around like cavemen.*

A picture of a ruined castle caught my eye and I read the accompanying text.

"While visiting the area, be sure to take a trip to the nearby ruins of Dunluce Castle, which sit on the edge of a cliff between Portballintrae and Portrush. The castle was the main stronghold of the MacDonnell chiefs of Antrim." Out of habit I reached for my phone to Google the MacDonnells, but the 'no-service' icon reminded me I needed a new sim card. I'd have to read up on the history later. Instead I put the breakfast away, washed my plate and poked my head out the front door. I blinked in the sudden brightness, but then my eyes widened in wonder.

We'd arrived home after dark and I didn't get a proper look around. Aedan's house was just outside the main village, an older building perched on a grassy knoll with an unbroken view of the sea. It was far enough away that the sound of the ocean wasn't deafening, nor the wind ferocious, but the deep sea-green horizon sliced in half by a merry blue sky with fluffy white clouds took my breath away. I felt refreshed by the salty sea air.

I realized I was basically living in a town other people visited on vacation. *This might not be so bad.* After I'd had my fill of the view, I turned to see a lady's bicycle leaned up against the house with a big purple ribbon tied to it.

The white paint was chipped and it was a little beat up, but it had a lovely woven basket tied to the front. I checked the tires and the brakes and everything seemed in good working order—I noticed the gears had recently been oiled. I hadn't ridden a bicycle in years, but it seemed like the right way to get around.

But I wasn't quite ready to stray from the house.

"This was your mother's room," Aedan had told me the night before, showing me into a small but cozy room with a desk, bed and chest of drawers. "It'll be yours now."

When he caught me staring at the boxes stacked in the corner, he said, "I never got around to packing up your mother's things after she left." Then he scratched the back of his head. "I guess I was too sentimental, and I liked feeling like she had a home she could come back to. When they got in touch with me... I put everything into the boxes, but thought you might want to keep something. I'll let you look through them."

I noticed the sadness in his eyes. I'd assumed there was a falling out of some kind—after all, normal teenage girls don't leave their families and move to the other side of the world without some cause. All I knew about my mom's childhood was that her mother died when she was very young, and she came to America years later, with no money and only a small suitcase. She was putting herself through nursing school when she met my father. He was brought in with a dislocated shoulder after a biking accident. "Love at first sight," Dad said. But I didn't know what was true anymore. Was there more to the story? And what other secrets did my mother hide from me about her past?

I brought my suitcases into the room and started unpacking. I set up my laptop on the desk and put the books I'd brought on the shelf above it. I probably brought too many, but they seemed really important at the time. Moby Dick, The Count of Monte Cristo, 20,000 Leagues Under the Sea, Robinson Crusoe, The Tempest. I realized suddenly that they were all stories about ocean adventures. My fascination with the sea probably came from my lack of personal experience. Mom always kept us as far away from saltwater as possible.

I put my clothes in the dresser and moved things around a bit more, then I finally pulled out my typewriter, and heaved it up onto the desk. My fingers twitched, aching to use it. I let myself caress the keys, but pulled away, staring instead at the boxes of my mother's things. I didn't get very far before the profound emptiness swelled up in my heart again, and I lost myself in tears.

When I finally tired of crying, I reached into the box with trembling fingers, and started pulling out items from the life my mother had abandoned before I was born. There were schoolbooks, a package of watercolors, a poster of an Irish rock band, a collection of coasters from different bars in Ireland, a chess set, an assortment of clothes and an old school uniform. There was also a walkman and a stack of tapes. The only band I recognized was the Cranberries, so I popped that in and put on the headphones.

Then I found the photo albums, and an old instant camera. I'd never seen pictures of my mom when she was this young before. I recognized her jet black hair and dark eyes, laughing and smiling with other kids I didn't recognize. But there were no punk clothes or spiked collars, or any other signs of teenage angst. The only thing that even hinted at rebellion was a tube of bright red lipstick. Nothing indicated that she wasn't happy.

Why did she leave?

One photo in particular stood out. There were four kids; a tall blond girl on the far left, a shorter, sandy-haired boy with a serious look, my mother in the middle, and a handsome, dark haired boy next to her on the right. I looked closer and saw he had one arm around her waist. A boyfriend? *Maybe Aeden had nothing to do with it.* I found some tape in the box and put the photograph up above the desk.

I read a lot of Nancy Drew and Hardy Boys books when I was younger, probably because my mother could pick them up for about a nickel at garage sales. I never considered myself a sleuth or kid detective, at least not since I'd turned eleven and started taking private singing lessons, but I picked up some habits that had stuck. Like making lists. And solving the mystery of my mother's secret past seemed like something to occupy my time; something which, since I didn't have any friends here, I would probably have a lot of.

I turned on my laptop and opened a new text file.

TO DO

1. Identify the kids in the photo

2. Ask them to tell me more about my mother and why she left Ireland

I paused for a few moments before adding,

3. Stop being angry at everyone who tries to make me feel better

4. Find the music department and keep practicing

I also opened up the document I used for my diary—a sprawling file of a few hundred thousand words that I'd updated almost daily since I was fourteen. But I wasn't sure what to write. I realized with a start that my mom probably kept a diary as well, so I ran over and rummaged through the box again. Then I checked all the drawers of the desk, under the bed and mattress, and all the other hiding places afforded by the room. *Nothing.*

Then I felt the darkness creeping in again. The fatigue, the emptiness. Rather than let it engulf me, I forced myself to get up and go outside. It was early afternoon. The buildings glowed a warm yellow, the sky was a pastel blue, and the Cranberries crooned in my ears.

Keep moving. Stay busy.

I jumped on the bike and pushed off down the road, riding wobbly at first. I hadn't been on a bike in years. In middle and high school it was cooler to walk to school than ride a bike. Portballintrae unfolded before me as I coasted down the road. There were a lot of new developments and orderly rows of cookie-cutter houses, but they weren't unpleasant to look at. I couldn't get over the incredible view of the teal-blue sea, framed by puffy white clouds and dark jagged rocks along the coast. I passed through 'downtown'—which consisted of one main street of shops and restaurants. It had the quiet elegance of a tourist town in off season. Business must be slow the rest of the year. On the other side of town I stopped to look at a field with some large circular bumps. They looked ancient. Remnants of some druid settlement, I guessed. The orderly lines of houses ended abruptly when I reached the far side of town, and there was a parking lot at the end of Beach Road with a lookout point. I sat for a while at one of three picnic tables, set out in the open, not twenty yards from the water, watching a handful of dark colored birds chase each other across the sky.

Then I took my shoes off and walked down to the beach. The sand squishing beneath my toes and smell of salt water brought a memory rushing back to me. It was one of my earliest memories, my only memory of the ocean, and the worst day of my life—the day I'd almost drowned. I'd never fully forgotten it, but had also never remembered it with much clarity.

My mother always tried to steer us away from the sea, but my father wanted me to experience the unique wildness of the Oregon coast, and took us on a surprise trip when I was five. I remember making a sand castle with a moat around it, and climbing over the rocks with my dad as my mother watched from a blanket nearby. We stuck our fingers in the sea anemones and chased the tiny crabs back into their holes. I was watching the water ebb and flow into the rock formations, gleefully surprised when it burst up suddenly and splashed me with water. But then a larger wave crashed over the rocks and wrapped around me like a giant hand, pulling me into the sea. It happened so fast, my dad didn't have time to grab me. I went rushing out into the deeper water, the dreadful silence pounding in my ears, my flailing arms cut up by the sharp rocks as I was dragged, terrified, along the bottom.

I remember feeling the undertow: overwhelming and inescapable. It pulled me into the deeper waters, the dark vastness, with a force greater than any I'd ever known. Sometimes I would fight to the surface and get a glimpse of the land slipping farther and farther away. I'd take a quick breath, and scream. I was exhausted from fighting, but just when I was about to give up, my father grabbed my arm and then side-stroked us back to land. He hauled me onto the rocks, and patted my back as I coughed up water.

Through my tears and the salt water I saw my mother running towards us. I held up my little arms to her, seeking comfort. Instead, she slapped me hard across the face. Then she grabbed my shoulders, staring at me with wild eyes and saying, "Never go into the sea again, do you hear me? *Never.*"

Much later, she apologized and said she was just so terrified when I disappeared, she didn't know how to react. I tucked the incident away, and we never talked about it again, but the unfairness of that slap was like a piece of sand in a clam shell. Something rough and uncomfortable, something I tried to cover up by making my mother love me more.

Now I felt like I was drowning all over again. I touched my palm to my cheek where she'd slapped me, wondering suddenly if there was more to the story. I tried to think of other incidents that might show my mother had been unstable, but came up blank. Apart from that one time, she'd always been completely in control. Dad's favorite term of endearment for her was 'my little ball of yarn.' As in *tightly wound.* The sun was setting and I started to feel creeped out, like someone was watching me. I looked around but I was totally alone, which creeped me out even more. So I grabbed the bike and started pedaling back to Aedan's place.

4

"Go ahead," Jackie laughed. "You're not in the U.S. anymore. Underage drinking isn't a big deal here, at least not for us. And anyway you've only got a few more years until you're eighteen."

After the beach, I'd cycled home and taken a shower, then pulled on some fresh, albeit travel-wrinkled clothes. I hadn't thought to bring any formal clothes with me, so I was wearing jeans and a black sweater.

Aedan and I walked down to his friend Liam's pub (I looked for a sign with the pub's name, but there wasn't one; just a little neon light in the window that said 'pub'). He introduced me to Jackie—the neighbor he'd mentioned. She was also the international school president, a grand title for a group she confessed included only two exchange students and me: a transfer from the USA.

We'd slipped into one of the corner tables. The bar was small but cozy, with gleaming wood counters and dark leather furniture.

The wall lamps cast a warm glow over an assortment of framed prints and news clippings, and a splash of green from the glass coasters completed the Irish theme. It smelled like hops and wood polish.

I must have looked unsure as I pondered the menu, so Jackie called over my shoulder for two half pints of Guinness. Jackie was thin and elegant, like my mother, moving with precision and self-control that seemed both wonderful and alien to me.

"So Aedan wanted me to explain our school system to you," she said. I couldn't help admiring her gorgeous, curly red hair that bounced when she spoke. She had deep blue eyes, flawless skin with perfect red circles on her cheeks (which was probably well-applied blush, but could just have easily have been caused by hiking up towards the pub in her black dress and heels).

"First, second and third year is the Junior cycle. After the third year we take a test to get our Junior Certificate—you'll need to take it at the end of this year. Next year, after you pass, we'll be together in the Senior Cycle, which is Fifth Year and Sixth Year. Then there's another big exam, and then we get a Leaving Certificate."

I nodded, trying to pay attention, but most of it slipped in one ear and out the other. I was having trouble thinking through to the end of the week. Next year seemed as tangible as the Easter Bunny. Plus, I had to strain to understand Jackie through her Irish accent, which was even stronger than Aedan's.

"You can take the bus with me on Monday," Jackie continued, "There are about fifteen of us from town, most of the students are from Portrush or Ballymoney. This one is Derry!" she said, as an older looking boy with broad shoulders set our beer on the table.

He was wearing a tasteful plaid button-down, and his sandy-brown hair was combed neatly to one side. He smiled and reached out his hand. I shook his hand and smiled back at him.

"Hi, I'm Clara."

"'Course you are, love," he said with a grin. "And let me say how sorry we all are… about your parents." Jackie shot him an apprehensive look and then glanced at me. Was it rude to bring up someone's dead parents after just meeting them? I didn't know either, so I wasn't sure how to react.

Jackie reached across the table and squeezed my hand. "If you ever need to talk about anything, you know, I'm here for you. I hope we'll be great friends."

"Thanks," I murmured, taking a moment to look Jackie and Derry in the eye, a gesture I hoped conveyed my sincere appreciation. I took a sip of my drink; it was so bitter I made a face to keep from spitting it out.

"Well, now you can say you've tried our national drink," Derry said, grinning. "Next time, get a hard cider."

Aedan had been chatting with Liam at the bar, but he came back to the table and put a hand on Derry's shoulder.

"I know you had a funeral in America for your parents, but in Ireland we do things a little different with a Wake; it's a kind of glorious send off for the deceased. I'd be a lousy father if I didn't give Branna a proper one, so I've asked some of the guys from town to play some music tonight."

Jackie took over the explanation, "It might seem strange to you, but the idea is to purge your sorrows with alcohol and exhilaration. Rather than let it stew and fester in solitude and quiet, we let it all out in one night, of singing and dancing, crying and mourning. It can get a little crazy. You can just watch, or join in, or do whatever you're comfortable with. Just remember we're not celebrating because we're happy they're gone, we're celebrating because they lived and we loved them."

Her last words touched a chord and my eyes watered.

As the pub filled with people, I looked around with new appreciation. This had been my mother's *home*. She lived here until she was sixteen. Many of the people in this room had been her neighbors or classmates.

"I didn't realize," I said, "that my mother still had... people here. Who cared about her."

My fingers dug into my pocket, where I had the photograph I'd found of my mother and her friends. I'd been hoping to ask Jackie and Derry about it, but with Aedan hovering nearby I wasn't ready to pull it out.

The band had been warming up in the background, and now they broke into a fast paced Irish jingle. With the music it was too noisy to talk, so instead I just kept an eye out for the faces in the photograph. Some of the couples started dancing, and chairs and tables were pushed back to make more room.

Our table was squeezed into the corner. As the night went on people kept coming up to me, telling me how they knew my mother and sharing anecdotes about her life. They brought food as well, and soon the table was overflowing with baked pies, cookies and casseroles. The older ones, Aedan's age, had known my grandmother Phyllis as well. Apparently she was quite the beauty. One gentleman, who must have been seventy-five at least, told me that Phyllis used to sing at the pub every Saturday night, and he'd been there in the front row, without fail, for three years to listen to her.

"The most incredible voice I ever heard," he said. "Could bring a grown man to his knees in tears. It was unearthly, magical. I've never heard anything like it since. Young Branna tried as she grew up to fill her mother's place, and she had a mighty fine voice as well, but nothing could compare to her mother."

"I didn't know my mother sang," I said, though now that I thought about it, I had vague memories of lullabies when I was very little. Suddenly my interest in opera music didn't seem so random. I knew almost nothing about my grandmother, and made a mental note to find out more about her.

At one point Jackie surprised me by getting up on stage to sing. Later Derry joined her in a duet. Some songs were slow and wailing, others made feet tap and my heart race. I don't remember when I started dancing, probably after my second Guinness (the taste had grown on me... it was like bread and chocolate). Then the room was spinning and I was hugging people, and crying—all at the same time, in a blur of warm orange lights and friendly faces and music that touched my soul.

I was a mess, but it felt amazing. I couldn't remember the last time I'd really let go like this. I always tried to hold my feelings in, but since my parents died, I'd been running out of space. I felt like a shaken soda bottle; full of sweetness inside but too pressurized to let anybody take the cap off. I was always afraid I'd explode, and somebody would get hurt. The alcohol poked holes in my stoic exterior. I'd been shaken, and was now fizzing out all over the place. For the first time in a long time, even before the accident, I felt part of a community. I felt accepted, and loved.

Even though everything was totally new and unfamiliar, I felt like I'd come home.

Then I noticed a face in the crowd I recognized. Dark, brooding eyes, under a set of furled black eyebrows with creases between them—staring at me with such malice my breath caught in my chest. We locked eyes, and then I tore the photograph from my pocket, certain he would match up with the laughing figure next to my mother. But when I looked up again he was gone.

I pushed through the crowd, eager to find out more about my mother but also a little afraid. Whoever the man was, he looked like he hated me. What had I ever done to him? Or, better question, what had my mother done? But after checking every corner of the bar, I still couldn't find him. *Had I imagined it?*

The bar felt warm and stuffy now, and my skin crawled, so I stepped outside. The air was crisp and chilly. I looked up and down the road but it was quiet and dark. *He couldn't have just vanished.* The door opened behind me with a loud creak that made my heart jump.

"Bit of fresh air, eh? Great idea—" Derry cut off as Jackie came up beside me and saw my face.

"What happened?" she asked, grabbing my arm. "You look like you've seen a ghost."

"A ghost, I don't think so. A man…"

I raised the photograph up for them to see.

"What's this?" Jackie asked, taking the picture from me.

"A photograph of my mom and some of her friends. I found it in her room. I thought one of them could tell me what happened to her, why she left."

"She never told you? Were you not close?"

Before last week I'd always thought we were.

"This is going to sound a little crazy," I said, "but she lied about where she was from, and even what her last name was. I never knew she was from Ireland, or that I had a grandfather here, until a week ago. So I'm just trying to... make sense of a confusing situation."

Jackie looked shocked but took it in stride, nodding. "Don't worry, we'll help in any way we can, right Derry?" She nudged him. "So you're looking for the kids in the photograph, and tonight you saw..."

"I don't know for sure. I saw a man, I thought he could be this boy next to my mother. Same features, dark hair and eyes... and he looked at me, right at me. Like he knew me. But then he disappeared."

"Well if he was here tonight someone will know him," Derry said, "Small town and all, no secrets here." Derry stood in the streetlight, and ran his hand through his hair. Suddenly I gasped and grabbed the photograph back from Jackie.

"This one," I said, pointing at the boy on the left of my mother, "looks just like you." I pointed at him. He took the photo.

"That's my Pa, Liam, you met him tonight," Derry said.

"And you didn't tell me he was friends with my mom?" I asked, not bothering to hide the accusation. My emotions were still muddled with the alcohol, and for a second it felt like everybody was keeping secrets from me.

Derry held up his hands, defensively, "I didn't know how close they were—and I didn't know you were hunting down her friends until a moment ago."

I leaned against the cool stone wall outside the pub and took a deep breath, trying to slow my racing heart. Suddenly I didn't like the feeling of alcohol in my stomach. I felt sick and dizzy. I wished I hadn't left my coat inside.

"I'm sorry," I said, "I'm just a little shaken up. I don't know why, but that guy inside, he didn't look like he'd come to bring an apple pie."

"We can go back to the pub sometime this week and ask Liam to talk to you." Jackie decided. "That will be the easiest way to start. I'm sure he can tell you who the other kids in the photograph were, and maybe even what happened with your mum."

"Sure you could," Derry said. "Though I'm not sure what he can tell you."

"What do you mean?" I asked.

"From what I can make of it, your mother started acting strange, grew apart from her friends. I don't think she had much contact with my Da for several months. Then she disappeared like. Ran off to America."

"It's still better to start with Liam," Jackie said, "and keep things quiet."

"What do you mean?" I asked. The chilly air outside the pub made me shiver, and goose pimples prickled my arms.

"Well it wouldn't look right for you to turn up after all these years asking questions. I mean, probably it's nothing, your mom ran away from home and nobody knows why. It's natural you'd want to look up her friends and find out more about her childhood. But assuming you're not imagining your tall dark stranger, or the drink is making you paranoid, there's another possibility—something happened to her that scared her away. And maybe that something is still here."

That's ridiculous. Jackie was being overly dramatic. I'd literally just arrived. I couldn't be in any real danger, could I? I went back inside to grab my coat, and told Aedan I was going to walk home. He wanted to come with me but I assured him I was fine. Portballintrae was so small I could walk from one end to the other in ten minutes. There's no way I could get lost. Jackie and Derry walked me out, and I said goodbye to them both with a hug. Normally I would have been self-conscious, especially with Derry—a strong, good looking guy—but somehow the drinking and dancing had melted my protective shell and I felt like we were old friends.

The adrenaline had subsided and now I was feeling the alcohol in a different way; a little dizzy, and a little sick to my stomach. The emotional high I'd been on had left me feeling very low, and I was horrified I might have made a fool of myself at my mom's Wake. I vowed to be more careful with alcohol from now on.

I barely registered the note pinned to the front door, I just grabbed it and let myself in. I stumbled to my bed and flopped down. The room tilted and I felt like I was on a flying saucer; everything was still moving and spinning around.

Then I glanced at the note. The paper was thick, and rough. Almost organic. The edges were black, as if they'd been singed with flame. The words were scrawled in an elegant, loopy script. I squinted to read it in the dim light.

Ashes to ashes, dust to dust,
beware the dangers,

return untouched.

Great, I thought. A threat. Or maybe a warning.

I thought the hard part of moving to Portballintrae would be the loneliness of starting over from scratch, but on my second day here, it looked like I already had more than my fair share of friends, and enemies. If only I knew which was which.

5

I woke up with the note clenched in my hand, and my heart started pounding as soon as my brain was clear enough to worry about it. Was that note meant for me? It said to 'beware the dangers'... but I had just gotten here. How could I be in any danger? I stuffed the note into my desk drawer and vowed to deal with it later. I felt gross, so I took a shower and brushed my teeth, then put on some jeans and a T-shirt. As a final touch, I wrapped the red ribbon around my wrist again. It looked silly, but I didn't want to remove it, so I pulled a sweater on to hide it.

Aedan greeted me when I came out of my room, and pulled a chair out for me at the table. Miscreant eyed me with disdain from the sofa. After a breakfast of eggs, bacon, coffee and two Aspirin—Aedan's foolproof hangover cure—we drove into Portrush. It was a much bigger town than Portballintrae. Aedan pointed out the mall, the movie theatre, and even a dance club as we drove by. After we parked, I pulled out the shopping list Aedan had picked up from the school.

Navy blazer with school badge
Grey skirt or grey trousers (available only from suppliers)
Skirts will be essential for specific occasions as decided by the school. Skirts must be of regulation type.
Navy v-neck pullover with school colours (compulsory for ALL pupils)
Plain white blouse
School tie
Navy or black tights or grey socks
Plain, low heeled black leather shoes, not trainers (if laced, laces should be black)
Optional:
Plain navy or black school coat (no badges, patterns, designs, lettering or other colours)

Aedan needed to pick up some painting supplies from the hardware store, so he gave me some money and dropped me in front of the department store. I browsed through the clothes and picked up everything I could find from the list.

A girl about my age was texting on her phone behind the desk. Her dark hair fell into perfect little curls. She was cute, except for her posture, which was hunched over the phone like a troll.

"Excuse me?" I said, trying to get her attention.

She ignored me. "Dressing rooms?" I tried again, a little louder. She sighed. Without glancing up to look at me, she pointed to her left, and I could see a small unmarked door.

In the dressing room, I tried on the basic outfit: skirt, plain white blouse, black leather shoes, navy V-neck sweater. I looked like I was going to a job interview. Then I tried on the tie and jacket. Now I looked like a Hogwarts student; all I needed was a magic wand.

My hair wasn't coal-black like my mother's, but it was still pretty dark, with hints of auburn. Unlike Jackie's, my curls were unruly and tangled, sticking out in random and distracting ways. I liked the way it accented my eyes, which were light blue, and contrasted with my dark eyebrows, but I wished it was more manageable. It went down past my shoulders, but I could always put it up if I had to. The school didn't have any special regulations for hair so I didn't worry about getting it cut.

I tugged at the constricting collar, and tried not to think about arriving at a new school tomorrow feeling ridiculous in these clothes. Dwelling on it wouldn't make it any easier. I felt much better after I'd changed back into my own clothes, and laced up my blue Doc Martens. With my arms full of clothes, I went back to the front counter, where shopgirl was still texting. Her long plastic fingernails made clicking noises against the screen of her phone.

"I'd like to buy these," I said, after standing there patiently for a few moments. Maybe she hadn't seen me. She held up her index finger, signaling me to wait while she finished her text. My arms were starting to tire when she finally put her phone away and rang up the clothing. The cash register showed the total and I put down a couple bills. She got out my change and plopped it on the counter. I'd given her Euro, but the change she gave me back were in pounds sterling. I picked up the foreign currency and tried to make sense of it.

"You slow or something?" she said, openly hostile.

"No I'm just… American," I said, my cheeks flushed in embarrassment.

"Same difference," she smirked, then went back to her cell phone. *What was her problem?*

I let the door slam in anger as I left the store.

Aedan was waiting for me outside, and we walked down the street to a stationery store. We bought pens, pencils, a ruler, a variety of notebooks for different subjects—and also a local sim card for my phone so I could finally get online. I spent the first ten minutes trying to walk and check Facebook and Instagram at the same time, until I tripped over a curb and nearly flattened myself. Then I put the phone away.

While in town I'd kept my eyes peeled for other familiar faces I could match to the photograph. I'm not sure why I didn't just ask Aedan; I'm sure he would have known who my mom's friends were. But we hadn't talked about my mom yet and it seemed like a sensitive subject. I didn't want to upset him.

On the way back to Portballintrae, Aedan stopped to show me Dunluce Castle. The crumbling stone walls perched on a cliff overlooking the sea felt like something out of a fairy tale. We had to cross a narrow bridge over a dangerous looking drop to reach the ruins. There was a small welcome area with a museum, where we bought tickets. A sign told me that the castle now had a smart phone app with an Audio Guided Tour. I tried out my internet connection by downloading the app. I didn't have earphones with me so I just held the speakers up to my ear.

"Dunluce Castle is located dramatically close to a headland that plunges straight into the sea, along the North Antrim coast, and was the headquarters of the MacDonnell Clan.

"There is archaeological evidence of a village that surrounded the castle which was destroyed by fire in 1641. The site was also witness to the sinking of a colony ship that broke up on the rocks off Islay in 1857 with the loss of 240 lives.

"Constantly fought over, it eventually succumbed to the power of nature, when the kitchen fell into the sea one stormy night in 1639. Reportedly, only one boy from the whole kitchen staff survived. After that, the owners refused to live in it anymore, and it was abandoned shortly afterward."

I walked around the ruins, exploring each little nook, trying to find perfect angles to capture both the entirety of the castle ruins and the stunning sea view behind it. My camera couldn't do it justice, so after a while I stopped trying and just soaked it up. Aedan gave me a lot of space to explore. I found a hidden corner and sat down against the ancient walls, trying to imagine what it would have been like to live here four hundred years ago. A short while later, Aedan found me, and we sat together, watching the sea.

"Your mom loved it here. It was her favorite place," he said.

"My mom came here?" I pictured my mother, the young beauty in the photograph, running through the ruins, maybe even sitting in this same spot.

"What was she like when she was younger?" I blurted, no longer able to curb my curiosity.

Aedan's eyes lit up and he smiled. "A lively one. Always singing and dancing and laughing. Always causing trouble. Wouldn't let anyone tell her what to do. She skipped school more often than I'd have liked, but it never seemed to hurt her grades. I was probably too easy on her though. Especially as a teenager, I didn't want to risk pushing her away. Seems like that didn't matter." This was the most we'd talked about my mom. *It was now or never.*

"What happened?" I asked suddenly. "I mean—why did she leave? She never talked about it here. Or about you."

Aedan sighed, gazing over the water. I wondered if I'd gone too far, if he was even going to answer, but after a while he spoke.

"She always had big dreams... I think she just got bored, you know, small town girl. She wanted more. Though honestly, I thought she loved it here. I never realized she wasn't happy."

But there was more—something else he wasn't telling me. I could see it in his eyes.

"Her mother, my wife Phyllis, left when she was four. It was just the two of us."

Phyllis *left?* Mom told me her mother *died* when she was four. I made a mental note to add that to my list of mysteries.

"I did the best I could. But it became more difficult, as she matured, when she became—"

He stopped, checking himself, and glanced over at me.

"When she became a woman. I didn't have all the answers for her. I wasn't enough."

His eyes started misting over. "She called sometimes, you know. Every year, for my birthday, to let me know how she was doing. Sent pictures of you sometimes."

"I didn't know that," I said. It seemed there was a lot I didn't know about my mother. I tried to imagine her, about my age, growing up here with Aedan in his house by the sea. I could see in his eyes, he loved her. Even though I didn't know him well, I didn't think he'd have done anything to hurt her.

But if it wasn't Aedan... why had my mother left Ireland? Did it have something to do with the strange man I'd seen? Did he leave that mysterious note, or was there another player? Or maybe it was all ancient history, and I was obsessing over nothing.

I had Aedan take a few pictures of me in front of the castle, and I posted a few on Facebook and Instagram. I also updated my status: *Thanks for all your comments and support. I'm adjusting to my new life here in Ireland. It's been hard, but I'll get through it.*

That night I went to bed early, knowing I'd have to get up for school the next day. I was glad Aedan had filled the weekend with activities, it kept my mind busy—too busy to feel the anxiety that was waiting for me as soon as I lay down. Things were moving so fast, it seemed like I had no control over my life anymore. I was nervous to be starting a new school in the morning, and though I tried not to admit it to myself, a small part of me was furious at my parents for leaving. I fell asleep thinking about the photograph, and all the questions I had about my mother and my grandmother.

***

I dreamt that I was floating across the ocean in a crystal sphere. The sound of the ocean grew louder, until it surrounded me, and I felt myself sinking deeper and deeper into it, until the surface was so far above me the light couldn't find me anymore. The waves pounding against the shore were in perfect sync with my heartbeat. I felt a chill and reached to pull my blanket up to cover me, but my fingers grasped at emptiness—it wasn't there.

Nor was my bed.

I opened my eyes frantically and gasped—I was standing in my pajamas at the very edge of a cliff, the white, foamy waves crashed against the rocks hundreds of feet below me. A sudden wind pushed me off balance, and for a second I teetered dangerously over the edge. I leaned back quickly and stumbled away from the precipice. The blood rushed to my ears and my legs trembled.

What the hell am I doing here?

I was halfway up the hill to Dunluce Castle, about fifty feet from the main road. I could see the silhouette of the castle off in the distance to my left, and the faint glow of lights from Portballintrae to the right, pulsing through a thin mist.

The full moon hovered in the starry sky, casting a wide, pearly gleam over glassy green water. A dark shadow I'm sure was a bat zipped past me with a leathery noise. As I surveyed the scene, a spot of white against the dark rocks below me caught my eye, and I gasped sharply when I peered down at it.

Impossibly, there was a boy down there, sitting on a small rock off the shore, looking up at me.

I blinked a few times and rubbed my eyes, but when I strained to get a closer look, I could still see him clearly. His face looked young, flawlessly smooth but with strong, perfect features. I would have guessed he was younger than me, except for his build, which—while lanky, had developed muscles. He almost looked like a marble statue, chiseled out of stone. His ash blond hair framed his face in wet, spiky tufts. But it was his eyes that captivated me the most. Somehow, even from this great distance, I could tell that they were light green, and almost iridescent.

If it were daytime I would have assumed he was posing for some kind of model shoot; he was leaning back on his hands casually, chin tilted up towards the moon as if absorbing its white rays. I leaned to the side to see the shoreline but didn't see any cameras. I looked back at the boy and realized I couldn't see his bathing suit. *Is he...? Oh my god, he's naked!* I thought I saw him smile, as if he could read my thoughts, and my cheeks flushed red.

Then I realized I was still in my pajamas, not to mention standing on the edge of a cliff like a lunatic. My feet were bare and now cut and dirty. When I looked again he'd vanished. A gust of wind made me shiver, and I wrapped my arms around myself. My curiosity was piqued, and I waited a few more minutes to see if he'd surface again. He didn't.

He's probably hiding. He's embarrassed some crazy girl caught him skinny dipping in the middle of the night. It's none of my business anyway. I laughed at myself, worrying about what some strange boy thought of me, rather than confronting the fact that I almost just killed myself sleep-walking off a cliff. Maybe I was losing my mind. Maybe I had a split personality and a whole alternate me was taking over my body, and doing things I couldn't remember. But if I *were* crazy, maybe there wasn't really even a boy down there at all. Maybe there hadn't been a scary looking man in the pub, either. *How can I tell what's real?* That thought terrified me, and I had a sudden and urgent need to be back at home in bed. Luckily there was only one road into town, and I was on it. I practically ran down the hill, crying out when I stumbled and skinned my knee on the cement road. I limped the rest of the way home and let myself in through the front door, which was, thank god, unlocked. Aedan hadn't noticed my absence, so I slipped into bed and tried—without success—to forget those mesmerizing green eyes.

6

The shrill beep of my alarm woke me, and I started getting ready for school on autopilot. It wasn't until I saw the blood on my knee that I remembered my midnight adventure. *So it was real.* But maybe parts of it had been a dream. I couldn't have really seen a boy out there. And anyway, so what if I had? I didn't have time to think about it right now. I took a shower and then combed the tangles out of my hair. I thought about putting on some makeup, but I couldn't remember if there were rules against that. I tried on my fake nerd glasses, which were kind of cool in America but might be really lame here. I hated the fact that I was so worried about my appearance. But it *was* my first day of school. In the end I decided to go *au naturel,* hoping that my unadorned plainness would help me disappear.

In the uniform, I could hardly recognize myself. It felt like I was disappearing; like somebody else had taken over my life. I grabbed the red ribbon from my desk and wrapped it around my wrist, tying the ends together in a small bow. With my jacket on, you couldn't see it, but somehow it made me feel stronger.

Jackie and Derry were waiting for the bus at the stop, and I joined them. It picked us up after a few minutes, and they introduced me to some friends of theirs. Derry was seventeen and in Fifth year. Jackie was my age, but in the transitional year, which is where I should be, but I'd be taking Third year coursework to catch up. While most students stayed in the same classroom, my schedule was erratic.

The only advantage was, even though it was a small school, the gossip lines didn't pass so easily between levels, so no one knew who I was, or that I'd just lost my parents. The sympathetic glances and whispers disappeared. People smiled at me and were friendly. I'd gotten so used to the sad looks I'd forgotten what it was like to be normal. Jackie dropped me off in the front office to check in and then left to run some other pre-class errands. I stood awkwardly waiting for the moon-faced lady behind the desk to look up and acknowledge me.

"Hiya, I'm Travis. Are you new this year?" said a voice behind me.

I glanced over my shoulder at a younger boy with sandy red hair and freckles. After I established he was really talking to me, I turned back to him and nodded.

"First day, can you tell?"

"You're American?" he said, raising his eyebrows in surprise.

"Is it so obvious?" I asked, looking down at my uniform, afraid I'd gotten something wrong. I tugged at the hem of my skirt, the draft on my legs making me feel naked and vulnerable.

"It's the accent that gives it away." His mischievous grin made me nervous. Just then the woman in the office looked at me over her spectacles. The plate on her desk said *Mrs. Weavers*. "Ah, Miss Clark, isn't it?"

I was suddenly grateful for my last name; I'm not sure why but I felt protected by that last bit of anonymity. I realized she was waiting for me to respond so I nodded, a little too eagerly.

"Here's your class schedule, love." She had gray hair and a pouty mouth, that she somehow managed to make look lascivious, as if she had just shared a dirty joke with me.

I reached out and took the schedule. She turned back to her computer and I headed into the hall, but then I heard behind me, "Travis, why don't you show Miss Clark to her classes?" Travis put on a dopey grin, obviously pleased to act as a tour guide. I wasn't sure if I should be flattered or if I just had the fascination of something new and unusual in such a small community.

The high school was small and mostly modern, though Travis told me there were parts of the building that were over one hundred years old. The small chapel at the back was built even earlier—it was used on special prayer days, but otherwise mostly just for couples to make out in, or "snog" as he called it.

Travis was a third year, just under me and Jackie, and a member of the chess club. I knew this about him, as well as what he brought for lunch and the names of all of his siblings, in the first five minutes. But I was happy to let him talk. He was fourteen but had the eager enthusiasm of a ten-year-old. Or maybe people were just less shy and awkward in Ireland than their teenage counterparts in America.

As we walked around I tried to get him to show me where my other classes were and made notes in my binder so I would remember. The schedule changed a bit day to day, but my main classes would be History, Geography, Modern Languages, English, Music, Drama, PE, Art and Design, Technology and Religious Education. I wasn't sure how I felt about that last one but I wasn't going to make a big deal out of it.

Mostly I wanted to keep my head down and not draw any unnecessary attention to myself. I learned quickly I needed to keep my mouth shut, as heads swiveled after us whenever I said anything to Travis and the hall resounded with my American accent.

"I can show you to your next room after class. Should I wait for you?" Travis asked hopefully. I hesitated, feeling the need to set boundaries and make it to my other classes on my own. I didn't know anything about the popularity hierarchy here, but hanging out with eager young chess players probably wouldn't score me any points.

Just then a girl with dark frizzy hair came over. I was pretty sure her long gold hoop earrings went against the dress code. "Beat it rugrat," she said to Travis. Then she turned to me, ignoring him completely, "Clara, is it?" She looked me up and down. "I'm Patricia, this is my beau Kyle." She nodded at the tall, dark skinned boy next to her. "I promised Jackie I'd keep an eye on you this morning."

"Oh... okay," I said. While my uniform hung off my skinny frame, Patricia's clung to her curvy body like plastic wrap. The top few buttons of her shirt were unbuttoned, and I caught Travis trying not to look at her cleavage.

I shrugged in apology to Travis and waved him off.

"Thanks Travis, you've been very helpful."

"Yeah, sure... well maybe I'll see you at lunch then." His shoulders slumped as he walked away. I felt a little bad for him, but I wasn't going to be rushed into a friendship with the first boy who talked to me.

"We are going to have to do something about your uniform," Patricia whispered to me as soon as we sat down in the classroom.

"Is something wrong with it?" I'd been very careful to follow the regulations. I even picked a skirt that was a little longer than necessary to hide my knees.

"No, nothing. It's perfect," she grinned. "Perfect for a goody-two-shoes, teacher's pet. But I've got a good feeling about you. You've got to show them they can't control you. You need to resist just a little bit to let people know you aren't afraid of the faculty." She gave me a conspiratorial wink and pulled out some safety pins.

I wasn't sure I was ready for a wardrobe makeover right in the middle of my first class. On the other hand, I didn't want to brand myself as a dork in my first few days by making the wrong first impression.

"I'm self-conscious enough wearing skirts to school," I said, stalling. "Can I have just a few days to get used to it?"

"Suit yourself," Patricia said, "but then I'm going to start taking up an inch every week until you get some sunlight on those thighs." She smiled wickedly. I blushed as Kyle ogled my lower body, and I wished my skirt went down to my ankles.

I made it through the morning without incident. The first teacher made me stand up and introduce myself as a new student, but thankfully the second teacher just ignored me and went about teaching as usual.

I chatted with kids sitting next to me, and Patricia introduced me to a few others. Riley, Kiara, Tristan... and more names I couldn't remember. The cliques seemed much tighter than they were in American high school—these kids had all known each other since they were little, most had been classmates for over ten years already. At the same time, strangely, people seemed nicer and more open with me than I'd expected. In an American high school, I'm pretty sure it would have taken weeks to make any friends.

After class, Patricia and Kyle walked me to the cafeteria. I saw Travis at a table waving at me, hopeful that I would come sit with him, but all the kids at his table looked about twelve years old.

Patricia grabbed me by the arm and steered me over to another table where I saw Jackie, sunlight on her fiery red hair and a pair of heart shaped glasses on her head. She looked perfectly at ease, and beautiful.

"How was your morning?" Jackie asked, peeling an orange.

"Fine," I said. "Patricia and the others have been really nice."

Derry joined us a few minutes later. While a lot of the other boys wore their uniforms in a slovenly fashion, loose and unkempt, Derry's was crisp and form-fitting. When he crossed the cafeteria he almost looked like he was strutting on a walkway. Patricia was off socializing and Kyle was talking to someone on the other side of the table, so Derry and Jackie and I ate together, chatting about our classes.

It was a few minutes before I realized something was off in the cafeteria. I saw hushed conversations and panic-stricken looks. At first I imagined people were sharing rumors about how my parents died. Or maybe some terrible history involving my mother or grandmother that I didn't even know about. But they weren't looking at me or sending glances in my direction. Whatever it was, it wasn't about me.

Patricia returned to our table and filled us in.

"Bedelia Meath disappeared this weekend," she said, leaning in close.

"She's missing?" Jackie asked.

"Left her house Saturday, all dressed up. Said she was going on a date. Wasn't anyone from school though—everybody's been talking but nobody saw her Saturday night. Never came home."

"The police waited forty-eight hours but put out a missing person's report this morning. They posted a copy in the main office, and they've been asking her friends questions."

"That's awful," Jackie said.

"Her parents have already started handing out flyers." Patricia reached into her pocket. She pulled out a photocopy with a picture of Bedelia, her details and a contact number. At that moment, two images flashed through my mind. The first was the dark-haired man I'd seen in the pub on Saturday night. The other was the mysterious blond boy I'd seen—or thought I'd seen—on the rocks.

Jackie shot me a look but didn't say anything. I knew she was also thinking about my dark stranger from the other night, but she was letting me decide whether or not to share. I shook my head. There was no way I wanted to get mixed up in rumors about a missing girl on my first day of school, but Patricia had already noticed our silent conversation.

"What?" she asked.

"It's nothing," I said.

"You two know something," her eyes widened.

Jackie reached for Patricia's hand, then looked at me. "This is probably an unrelated coincidence. You can't tell anybody else about it." Patricia nodded, and I sighed.

"My mother grew up in Portballintrae. She left when she was a teenager and I'm not sure why. I have a photograph of her with some friends, and I'm trying to track them down. On Saturday night I saw someone I thought could be one of the kids in the photograph, but he looked... *angry* with me. Like he wanted to hurt me."

Patricia's mouth hung open for a few seconds, then she said, "You've got to tell the police."

Derry interrupted, "We can't go to the police just because this guy gave Clara a mean look. Maybe he was just having a bad day or angry at something else. Maybe Clara misread it."

"Can I see the picture?" Patricia asked.

I pulled the photograph from my pocket, and as I did the note fell out too. Jackie picked it up, then paled slightly as she read it.

"What's this?" Jackie asked. "Where did this come from?"

Derry took it from her and read it as well. He let out a slow whistle.

"Found it on my front door, Saturday night after the Wake," I admitted. "I was going to show it to you..." But I wasn't actually certain I would have.

"It's just a strange note, it probably doesn't mean anything." Patricia took the note and read it out loud.

"*Ashes to ashes, dust to dust, beware the dangers, return untouched.* Someone pinned this to your front door?"

I nodded. With a girl missing, the note seemed especially ominous.

"Has Aedan seen this?" Derry asked.

"No." *And I want to keep it that way.* "I didn't think it meant anything..."

"But it sounds like a threat," Jackie said. "Maybe it wasn't even meant for you, maybe it was meant for Aedan."

I felt the blood draining from my face. "I hadn't thought about that." I suddenly felt like an idiot. "You think he's wrapped up in something?"

"If he is, keeping this message from him might not be a good idea."

I nodded, but wanted to distance myself from what was quickly becoming major drama.

"But, there's no way any of this stuff could have anything to do with me, right? I mean, I'm not even from here. Whatever is going on, wouldn't it be best to just stay out of it? I never even met Bedelia. There's no way this could be connected to her."

"I agree, it's probably nothing," Jackie said. "On the other hand, it's better to find out the truth and prove there is no connection, than to stick your head in the sand and be blindsided later. What if this note *does* have something to do with the missing girl, but you didn't bring it to the police, and they find out about it later?"

The hairs on my arm stood up. Jackie was right, though the thought of getting involved in a police investigation right now made me sick to my stomach. Sticking my head in the sand sounded like the perfect solution to me, or at least the most comfortable one.

I glanced at Derry. "Can we go to the pub tonight, and find out if Liam knows anything first? If he can tell me who the kids are in the photo, maybe it will help me figure out the rest." I wasn't sure why I didn't just ask Aedan, but teens didn't always share problems with their parents. If there was bad blood between my mom and her friends, Liam was more likely to know about it.

"Sure, we can stop by right after school," he said.

Jackie pursed her lips together but didn't say anything. I knew she was disappointed in me, but she didn't know what it was like to be a new student in a new school. I was trying hard not to be the center of gossip, which meant I needed to keep some cards to myself.

I chewed my lip however, thinking about what Jackie had said. Was I being stupid and selfish, by not volunteering a possible clue? Was this girl, Bedelia, in danger? I promised myself I'd make a decision after meeting with Liam, though my stomach was in knots for the rest of the day.

After lunch was English. The teacher's name was Justin Sadleir. He was young and kind of hot—at least that's the way Patricia described him just before heading into the classroom. I could see the appeal. He had dark hair and was wearing a blue shirt with a jacket and tie. He smiled at me when he handed me a list of the semester's books to read. I felt a little proud that I'd already read two thirds of them; famous works of classic literature. Most of the others I'd heard of, but never gotten around to. I also got a sheet describing the aims for the course, which were to *"Express personal reactions to or opinions about world events, discuss concepts relating to literature, communicate individual responses to poems and literature, and develop individuality as a reader by experiencing success and enhancement of self-esteem through reading."*

I soon learned that this meant a lot of group discussions and participation, something that frankly terrified me. But at least we were talking about books, and I loved books. I was able to follow the conversation and Mr. Sadleir didn't seem to pick on students mercilessly, unless they looked unprepared. I vowed to be prepared for class and finish all the readings ahead of time.

And then, finally, it was time for music class. I was excited to find the music room, which had always been a place of comfort for me, but I froze when I entered the classroom and saw a familiar face framed by dark curls—the rude shopgirl from Portrush. She looked away and pretended she hadn't noticed me.

"Clara," the teacher pulled me aside as I came in the door. "Welcome, I'm Mrs. Tierney. I heard you were quite the singer." She was wearing a simple gray sweater over a black dress, and had a pair of glasses hanging from her slender neck on a silver chain. Her hair was streaked with gray but her face was still smooth and young. "I'm really excited to have you in my class this year, and there are some competitions coming up we could really use you for. Why don't you just jump in wherever you want today, and we'll figure out where to put you later."

I nodded, grateful for the teacher's interest, though I'd planned on holding back for the first few days. Nobody liked a show off and my opera voice would probably be out of place in a high school choir.

"Roisin, can you scoot over so Clara can sit next to you?"

So that was her name. She looked me over with her clear blue eyes, and sneered. Maybe she didn't recognize me after all; she'd hardly looked at me in the shop.

"But I'm still lead soprano, right?" Roisin asked, with a hint of a whine.

"We'll reassign places in a few days, once we see where Clara fits." Mrs. Tierney said.

"But she'll have to audition to get a place." Roisin pouted, crossing her arms.

Exaggerated facial expressions had always rubbed me the wrong way. Maybe it's because I don't have any; my facial expressions betray my feelings and moods, I have trouble enough reigning them in. I'd never be able to have enough self-control to deliberately used practiced expressions.

"I'll just sit over there," I said, pointing to a chair on the far right. Mrs. Tierney frowned, but didn't force the issue. I breathed a sigh of relief. I didn't want to get into any politics on the first day, and I knew from experience musicians were protective of their placements, which signified ability. If Roisin had earned first chair, she had every right to be defensive of her space. That wasn't an excuse for being such a bitch on Saturday though.

I didn't care, anyway, I just wanted to sing. Since that moment when I saw the police and knew my parents were dead, the experience of singing had been broken for me. But I desperately wanted to put it back together. I was always happiest when singing, and I needed to feel happy again.

We sang a song I recognized, and then one I didn't, but I had no trouble reading the music. At first I held my voice in check, but with everybody singing together, I let go a little, breathing in deeply and pushing the notes from my stomach as I'd been taught. I noticed the other girls eyeing me and got quieter.

"Wonderful, WONDERFUL," Mrs. Tierney said, clapping her hands. Clara, you have a tremendous voice." Roisin turned and gave me dagger eyes. Guess she noticed me now.

The last period of the day was marked PE. I'd brought gym shorts, a white T-shirt and some tennis shoes, which I changed into when I finally found the gym. The other students had already started playing volleyball.

The teacher, Mr. Kearns, told me to call him Martin and added me into a rotation. I'm not particularly athletic, but I made an effort. Unfortunately that wasn't enough. These girls took sports seriously. They were all wearing knee and elbow pads and would dive for the ball almost every time it came over the net. When it came near me I stumbled towards it and tried to scoop it back up. I was successful about half the time. I soon got tired of apologizing every time I screwed up. The girls compensated by going for balls that should have been mine, not that I cared.

Then one ball went high and was coming down straight to me. I put my hands up to set it, but the girl on my left shoved me out of the way with her hips and hit it instead. I landed awkwardly on the ground, and rubbed my sore wrist.

"*Sorry.*" She flipped her hair off her shoulder. Roisin was on the other team, and I felt my cheeks flush as she stifled a laugh. My palms were moist and the tops of my ears burned as I picked myself up and shuffled back into position.

It's no big deal. I was in the way and I suck at sports. And I obviously didn't care about the game. But on the inside I was shaking with anger.

After class, I found Derry and Jackie waiting for the bus in the front of the school. Moments later Patricia came up and put an arm around me.

"I heard you got roughed up in gym class," she said.

"That literally just happened. Is nothing in this school a secret?"

"Gossip is the unofficial pastime here," Derry said with a smile.

"Anyway, it was nothing," I said, as Jackie gave me a worried look. "I'm sure it was an accident."

"Not likely, from the way Brianna and Roisin are going on about it."

She nodded over at the two girls, who were laughing and chatting with a group of boys not far away. Brianna must be the one who pushed me. She had long blond hair that she kept twirling with her finger. Roisin stood next to her, with her perfect dark curls and cute button nose. She looked like a porcelain doll. The kind that murdered you in your sleep.

"Want me to rough'em up for you?" Patricia asked, pantomiming rolling up her sleeves.

"Maybe just a black eye or bloody lip?" I joked, making the others laugh.

I suddenly felt grateful for my new friends. The first day of school was challenging, but it could have been worse. And I had more important things to think about. "Can we take a group photo?" I pulled out my phone. "To commemorate surviving my first day?"

We huddled together on the lawn. Derry, who had the longest arms, held the phone as we said, "Cheese."

I took the phone back and opened up the picture to check it. It was a fun picture, a bunch of smiling teens in school uniforms. I almost didn't recognize myself. I was about to post it to Instagram when something else caught my eye; a face in the background, watching us.

I spun around to look for the photobomber and found him easily—a small old man, with white hair and sun-soaked skin, holding a rake and a black plastic bag.

He was still staring—when I met his eyes he looked startled, and quickly looked away and went back to raking.

"Still looking for the kids in the photograph?" Jackie asked.

I realized my eyes *had* been searching faces all day, but not because of the photograph. My face turned red as I realized I was hoping to see the mysterious boy from the rocks. Even worse, I realized I was disappointed that I hadn't found him. If he was local, he *could* have gone to this high school. And if I found him, at least it would prove I wasn't going crazy. But from the way my heart was pounding, I don't think that was the only reason I wanted to see him again.

The bus pulled up across the street and I stepped off the curb towards it.

Suddenly I heard a loud screeching of brakes, and looked up to see a motorcycle swerving to miss me. It stopped just before it hit, but I stumbled backwards, frozen as I looked up at the driver's face. For a second I thought it was the dark man from the pub, and my heart pounded. The scowl was similar, but this guy was much younger, around my age. His long, dark hair spilled out from under his helmet. I was sure we'd never met before, but at the same time, he seemed intimately familiar to me somehow.

He pulled off his helmet and I saw he had a cleft in his chin, and a strong jaw. He looked like a Disney prince, but maybe the evil kind. He must have taken his jacket, shirt and tie off already; his V-neck shirt was mostly covered by a black leather jacket with a hood. His leather bracelets and combat boots looked out of place with his dress slacks.

He clenched his fists together, but then the angry expression eased from his face. He smirked at me with a spark of humor in his eyes. "If you wanted to get my attention, you could have just asked me out. No need to try and kill yourself."

As he spoke, he ran his fingers through his hair, and I saw the hint of a tattoo on his collarbone. I thought I caught a whiff of cologne, but it was subtle. It smelled natural and musky, like moss on old wood, or a campfire. I realized he was staring at me and waiting for me to say something.

"I'm... sorry," I stuttered. I wanted to yell at him, but I'd basically stepped right into the street without looking. I realized it was because they drove on the left here, and I wasn't expecting anyone to come in that direction. *Stupid.* I needed to be more careful from now on.

"Well then," he said, "Now that that's over, could you maybe get out of my feckin' way?"

My mouth dropped open. *Who was this asshole?*

"Never mind him," Jackie said, pushing me forward and glaring at the boy. "That's Ethan. Just a local dirtball."

"A *hot* dirtball," Patricia said under her breath as she walked past me.

Ethan gave a mock salute and winked at me, as he gunned his engine and rode off on his motorcycle. I tried to resist the urge to stare after him, but curiosity got the better of me. Patricia noticed my lingering gaze.

"Some of the girls call him Snape, because he's dark and brooding," she said. "And rumor has it he messes around with dark arts."

"What, like magic?" I scoffed.

At this, Jackie turned and placed a hand on my arm. "There may not be much magic in America," Jackie said, "but Ireland still has its fair share. You're in the land of leprechauns and fairies, now," she said. There was a mischievous gleam in her eye, but something told me she wasn't entirely joking.

7

I thought I'd have to beg Aedan to let me out of the house on a school night, especially my first school night, and to go to a *pub*— but I told him it was to meet Jackie and Derry, and he readily gave permission. I think he was happy I'd made friends and wasn't just moping around the house. I promised we'd just have soda, and he told me to be home by ten. I wondered if he'd have agreed so easily if he knew what I was going there to discuss.

I left the house at dusk and walked up the street, watching the golden hues of the sunset over the horizon. Even though I'd never met her, I couldn't stop thinking about Bedelia. What if the creep I saw Saturday night had something to do with her? What if he left the note? Was I withholding evidence? Was she in danger?

It was a Monday night, so the place was pretty quiet, though not entirely empty. I pulled off my purple scarf and set down my leather bag. I was wearing a baggy gray sweater, but decided to keep it on for a while. I took the red ribbon off my wrist and used it to tie my hair up into a pony tail. Tonight the bar smelled like cigar smoke. A couple of guys were playing darts on the other side of the bar.

When Derry told Liam I had some questions about my mom, he looked at me uneasily but agreed to sit down while Derry watched the counter. Liam was tall and lean, with round glasses and soft, copper-colored hair. He wore a black apron when he was working.

"So, Clara, how can I help you?"

"You and my mom were friends, right?" I asked.

"Good friends. Best of friends, for a long while."

"I just... wanted to know more about her childhood. She never talked about Ireland and I wanted to understand more about her life here."

Liam's face relaxed—he'd thought I was going to ask something else. *Something he didn't want to tell me.* I wondered how I could needle it out of him.

Derry brought his father a pint, and I watched Liam take a sip. He wiped his lips with a napkin, and then started talking.

"She was a happy child. Grew up a tomboy, on account of her mother being gone, you know." I wanted to interrupt and ask him what happened to my grandmother, but I let him continue instead. I'd have to ask more about that later.

"We were stupid kids. We'd dare each other, a group of us boys, to do risky things. Throwing rocks at a house to see who could get closest to the window without breaking it. Jumping between all the boats in the harbor without falling in. I wasn't nearly as brave as she was, or the other boys, and sometimes they'd pick on me, goading me to do something, and she'd just go and do it herself." His eyes lit up with the memories.

"We called her Raven, when we were young. That's what *Branna* means, you know. A beauty with hair as dark as a raven. It suited her. And she was so wild. Fearless. It was a good nickname."

He took another sip of his beer.

"When she was older, she started hearing the rumors about her mother's disappearance, and other kids teased her about it. Most of the boys were afraid to hit a girl, but they'd usually defend themselves after taking a few punches. Your mother's fists were legendary at our school." He smiled fondly.

"The rumors?" I prompted. This is what I needed to hear.

"Aye, I don't expect Aedan will have told you much about your grandmother," he said, with a worried expression.

"Just that she left when my mom was four," I said.

"I hardly think I should be the one repeating idle gossip," Liam said.

Derry had been listening in, and he put a hand on his father's shoulder.

"If not you, some kids at school will probably bring it up and start teasing her as well."

"True, true..." Liam sighed heavily.

"Please, I need to know the truth—or at least what people are saying," I said.

Liam exhaled slowly before continuing. "Your grandmother Phyllis was always a bit odd. Beautiful and enchanting, no question. But there was something that didn't seem real about her, like when you were in her presence, you'd fallen into a dream.

Every man in town would have walked through fire to be with her, but she loved Aedan. When she disappeared... she wasn't the only one. Father Murphy, the town priest, disappeared at the same time."

"Wait—what?" My pulse quickened. "They left together?"

"Nobody knows for certain. I was just a kid myself when it happened mind you, but I grew up with the rumors. She disappeared. The following Sunday there was no sermon. It took a couple weeks to find a replacement. Some folks said Phyllis had bewitched Fergus—Father Murphy. Some say Father Murphy went mad, killed her and then himself. Others say it was a suicide pact. But there were no bodies. The both of them just up and vanished."

"What do you think happened?" I asked.

"The funny thing is, when Phyllis went missing Aedan never filed a missing person's report with the police. Some people thought maybe he'd discovered Phyllis and Fergus together and offed them both—he'd never do that, of course. I don't doubt that he loved her, and she him, but he also wasn't very surprised that she'd left him. It was like he was always expecting her to leave."

My head was spinning with all this new information. My fingers twitched over imaginary keys, trying to write it down so I could sort it out later.

"So... my mom, Branna, grew up hearing these rumors about her mother?" I asked.

"Well, not entirely—after she bloodied the first couple of lads who brought it up, nobody would say it to her face. And kids our age, we had our own rumors and gossip to keep us occupied. But the older folks in town, they'd still look funny at her—especially when she got older."

"Why, what happened then?" I was on the edge of my seat, barely daring to breathe.

"Well, let's just say, as she turned into a young woman, she looked more like her mother. And it wasn't a gradual change. She went from a scrawny, wild little girl to a beautiful woman in the space of a few weeks. Some saw her transformation as supernatural. Men in town started turning their heads to watch her pass. The older folk remembered her mother and shook their heads, saying no good would come of it, clucking together like hens. Something should be done, they said."

My blood ran cold. *Something should be done?* These superstitious people in their backward little town were angry about my mom suddenly becoming too pretty? Had they done something to my mother that drove her away?

"I don't mind admitting I also had a crush on your mother," Liam continued. "She was always beautiful to me, even before the more obvious changes in her appearance. But she made other friends in high school, and we spent less time together."

I nodded, my ears perking up. This was important.

"Anyone in particular?" I asked.

"She started hanging out with one boy a lot. I was jealous. Sometimes I'd try to follow them, see what they were up to. She caught me once, and gave me a good talking to. And a black eye to boot."

"Who was the boy?" I asked.

"His name was Colin, Colin Blake."

"Is this him?" I pulled out the photograph. My fingers were almost trembling. I don't know why I was so excited, but it felt like I was on the verge of discovering something significant.

"Aye, that's him." Liam nodded, gesturing with his beer.

"Do you know where he is now? I thought I saw him here the other night," I said.

"You couldn't have," Liam said, his eyes darkening.

"Why not, did he move away?"

Liam took a long, slow sip of beer before responding.

"He died. Same day as your mother disappeared. Stabbed in the heart."

***

I sat in silence, stunned. Jackie put a hand to her mouth in surprise, and Derry's eyes were wide. None of us spoke for several moments. My grandmother seduced the town priest and disappeared mysteriously, and apparently my mother did practically the same thing years later—fleeing the country and leaving a dead body behind. It seemed like my family was cursed with tragedy. All the older people in town were going to hate me, those who knew who I really was.

But why did my mother run? Did she kill Colin? If not, what happened to him? Who was the strange man I saw, if not Colin, and why did he look so angry? For a fleeting second I wondered if it was Colin's ghost out for revenge, but ghosts don't leave handwritten messages stuck on doorways.

Was I in danger too? Or was I somehow a danger to others?

Before we left, Liam told me the name of the other girl in the photograph: *Barbara Dubbs*. If I could track her down, maybe she would have some more answers for me. We thanked Liam, and started walking back to Aedan's house. We'd successfully identified the four figures in the photograph, but it didn't feel like a victory. I was left with more questions than answers, and learning the truth about my mother's sudden exodus filled me with grief.

"Now what?" Derry asked, breaking the silence.

"None of this has any obvious connection with Bedelia," I said. "I don't see how sharing the note with anyone could help the investigation."

"I still think you should go to the police," Jackie said.

"And say what? The ghost of my mother's ex-boyfriend pinned a threat to my door? They'd lock me up."

"Let them figure out whether or not the information is relevant," Jackie said.

"I'm with Clara on this one," Derry said. "Maybe if there was some connection between Clara's family history and Bedelia, but I can't see any. They've never even met each other. We don't know that Clara is actually in any danger, or that the note is a threatening message. It could be a Bible verse for all we know; maybe they're getting pinned on lots of doors."

"It's not in the Bible," I said. "I looked it up. It's from the *Book of Common Prayer*. At least, the first half is."

"Anyway..." Derry continued, giving Jackie a look. "It seems like it should be her choice, not ours."

I was grateful that someone was on my side. "I want to try and find the last girl in the photograph first—Barbara Dubbs. Maybe she lives around here still. If anything else turns up or I feel like I'm in real danger, I promise I'll go to the police."

Jackie seemed to accept my decision, though she didn't agree with it. There was something else to feel guilty about though: my late night encounter with the blond boy. Although I had no idea whether he was involved in any of this (and the likelihood was improbable to say the least) he was the second mysterious man I'd run into, the same weekend as a girl disappeared. Not sharing that detail with my new friends felt like a significant omission.

8

There's a YouTube video of funny animal compilations I've watched dozens of times. In one of them, a giraffe is confronted by a peacock. The peacock spreads its colorful tail, and the giraffe is so surprised its legs all try running off in different directions. That's exactly how I felt when I saw water boy again, standing at the front of third period on my second day of school, his blond hair casually tousled like he'd just stepped out of the ocean. He was wearing a school uniform, like everybody else, but his presence seemed so out of place it derailed me completely.

I hadn't slept well; I couldn't stop thinking about Colin and my mother. I dozed through Geography and Technology (the former seemed useless since we all had Google Maps on our phones; the latter consisted of lessons in using software applications). And then suddenly, there he was. I was so surprised to see him, I dropped my notebook on the ground, then stooped and fumbled for it while blocking the influx of students. By the time I made it to my seat, my cheeks were burning. His eyes weren't as vivid as I'd remembered, but still very green. And he was staring at me with a bemused expression, as if daring me to ignore him.

"Class, we have another new student to welcome." I shrank in my seat, hoping he wouldn't single me out. "This is Sebastian. His family just moved here from…"

He paused and looked down at the paper he was reading from.

"A small town in Iceland," Sebastian offered, his voice much lower and deeper than I would have guessed. He had a very slight accent that was hard to place. "You wouldn't know it. And it's a beast to pronounce." He said this with a smirk, without taking his eyes off me. He definitely remembered me from the other night.

From close up, his features seemed otherworldly. He had high cheek bones, and his cheeks sunk in a little under them. His perfectly straight nose had a small bump on the upper part, and his jaw was lean and strong. My eyes were drawn to his round eyes, made prominent by dark lashes and graceful eyebrows, and his big, full lips, which made me think of kissing him. I tore my eyes away, my blush deepening. Yesterday I'd thought Mr. Sadleir was good looking, but standing next to Sebastian, he was unexceptional in every way.

What is he doing here? When I saw him the first night I assumed he was a local. But if he just moved here, why wasn't he at school Monday? Why is he only showing up now?

Mr. Sadleir was looking around for a place to put him.

Not by me not by me not by me—

"Well, Clara is new too, as it happens. Why don't you sit next to her for now?" Mr. Sadleir motioned to the empty seat next to me.

Sebastian sat to my left, stretching out his long legs and crossing them under the desk in front of him. He didn't take out any books or notes. Not even a pencil. Whatever he was here for, it wasn't an education. Mr. Sadleir started class and I tried to focus on what he was saying, but it may as well have been gibberish. I wasn't the only one having trouble concentrating; a group of girls on the other side of the classroom was whispering and fluttering their eyelids at Sebastian.

I looked over at him, finally, and found him staring directly at me. I panicked, wondering if I had something on my face. I wiped my hands on my skirt.

"Stop staring," I hissed at him.

He cocked an eyebrow and held his hands up defensively, before turning his eyes towards the front of the room. I couldn't shake the feeling that Sebastian's arrival wasn't a coincidence.

I mean, what did I know for sure? A hot guy shows up at my school, and just because I first saw him under unusual circumstances, I think—what, that he's following me? That he enrolled in this school and showed up in my English class to find out more about me? That's insane, right? I'm obviously delusional.

After what seemed like eternity, the bell rang and I was out of my seat like a shot.

Lunchtime.

I wanted the security of numbers. I grabbed Jackie when I saw her in the hall and linked arms with her. I didn't let go until I was seated at a lunch table with friends on all sides. A few minutes later I saw Sebastian saunter in, surrounded by the group of doe-eyed girls from my last class. Jackie saw me watching him and turned to look.

"Who's that?" she asked.

"No idea," I replied, focusing on my food.

"He's cute," she said. "And he's coming over here."

I choked on my sandwich and then took a huge sip of milk to wash it down, but missed my mouth. I was wiping the milk off my face and uniform with multiple napkins when he arrived.

"Mind if I join you?" he asked a few seconds later, looking at me with his gorgeous green eyes and a confident smile that he had no right wearing. The group of girls trailing after him seemed crushed, and wandered off slowly.

"There's no room—" I mumbled, my mouth still full of sandwich, but Jackie had already scooted over to make a place for him.

"I'm Jackie," she said, holding out her delicate, well-manicured fingers.

I hid my hands in my lap.

"Sebastian," he said.

"You're new," Jackie said.

"From Iceland," I offered.

Jackie glanced at me with a confused look.

"We had last period together."

"Oh, so you know each other already."

"Yes," Sebastian said, looking at me just as my lips were forming to say "No."

I realized I was being unfairly rude.

I'm not sure what it was about him that got my blood pumping.

He was a new student, like me. It was only natural for him to seek me out. Not to mention the shared secret of our bizarre midnight meeting. It's hard being the new kid. He probably just wanted to make some friends.

"What do you think of town so far?" I asked, pretending to be normal. Running from him hadn't worked in my favor. I'm sure once he got to know me he'd realize how boring I was and leave me alone.

"It's full of curious and surprising things," he said, without taking his eyes off me, his voice dripping with hidden meaning, or so I thought.

"Oh! You should join us this weekend," Jackie said. "Clara has only been here a few days as well, we're going to do a little sightseeing."

"That would be great," he said. "If it's not an imposition."

Imposition? Who talks like that?

"Facebook me," she said, pulling out her phone.

"Face-what?" he asked. For a second, he had me going, but then I caught the glimmer of humor in his eyes. His lips twitched as he tried to keep a straight face.

Cute.

He pulled out the latest iPhone and sent Jackie a friend invite.

I listened as Jackie made small talk with Sebastian, but everything about the situation seemed surreal. My brain screamed at me to pay attention. Something about Sebastian wasn't right. I didn't feel threatened, exactly. He didn't give me a creepy or dangerous vibe, like the guy in the pub had. But something told me to be cautious.

Then I figured it out: I was eating lunch with attractive people. Jackie was probably the cutest girl in the school, with Patricia a close second. Derry had that homegrown, boy-next-door appeal, and now Sebastian had joined us. Sebastian wasn't trying to fit in: he *belonged* here. He was just naturally gravitating towards his own social class. I was the one who didn't belong. And it wasn't just looks, these were kids with self-esteem and confidence that came from years of getting what they wanted. I was pretty, and reasonably attractive for my age, but I also had the normal teenage girl shortcomings: chronically low self-esteem, overanalyzing and thinking about everything, the almost painful social awkwardness. Problems that didn't seem to exist at this table.

Jackie suddenly laughed—a little too loudly—and put her hand on Sebastian's arm. I'd never seen her flirt so openly before. A tiny, irrational part of my brain felt betrayed.

Sebastian seemed to have this effect on every girl though, and for obvious reasons. He was so good-looking he was practically angelic.

Jackie glanced over at me and I saw the smile disappear from her face.

"I, um, have to go..." she said, looking at me curiously. "Catch up with you two after school. Sebastian, great to meet you."

I wanted to grab onto her arm and ask her to stay. She probably thought she was doing me a favor, leaving me alone with the new cute guy. *Maybe she thinks I like him.* Sebastian was looking at me expectantly. I searched for something clever to say, but under the intensity of his gaze, my whole body was desperate to get away. I got up from the table and headed across the cafeteria without a word.

He fell in step beside me.

"Fancy seeing you here," he said with raised eyebrows.

"Are you following me?" I asked, instantly regretting the harshness of my tone.

What is it about this guy that brings out the worst in me? Why couldn't I just flirt and banter like Jackie or Patricia? He reached in front of me and put his hand against the wall, blocking my path. He leaned in closer, inches from my face, and whispered, "Yes."

I stopped breathing.

Who the hell is this guy?

"I saw you... in the ocean," I said finally, my knees feeling wobbly. The space between us seemed to pulse with energy. He smelled like sunshine, lemon and lavender, and new clothes. My stomach was doing somersaults.

"And I saw you," he said. "Standing at the edge, the sea calling to you. I haven't seen one of your kind around for decades. I was... curious."

"My kind? *Decades?*" I pushed his arm away and stormed down the hallway. I wasn't sure what he meant, but it sounded insulting.

He caught up to me and grabbed my arm.

"I don't mean any offense. I just meant..." But then he stopped and looked at me in confusion. "You don't know..." he said, making me feel stupid. There was a trace of pity on his face; an expression I'd become very good at identifying in the last few weeks.

I *hated* pity.

I didn't need anybody else to pity me. Especially not this gorgeously annoying underwear model who swims naked in the middle of the night.

"I don't know what you're talking about," I said, whipping my arm out of his grasp.

He was acting much too familiar and intimate for some strange guy I didn't know at all. And what did he mean, he hadn't seen any of *my kind* for decades? He couldn't be much older than I was. I wanted to stick my head in a dark corner and hide, at least just to figure out what was going on. Not for the first time, I felt exposed in this uniform.

"I apologize," he said, his cockiness and playfulness gone—replaced by an emotionless mask. "It's just that I... I want to know more about you. Can we meet after school?" Something about his eyes soothed me, and I ached to give in to his request.

"I have to go," I mumbled instead, pushing past him.

I thought he'd run after me again, and I was expecting to feel his grip on my elbow.

It never came.

I wanted to leave school, but the day wasn't over yet, so I had to suck it up. I set out with no plan other than to avoid other people, and soon found myself at the back of the school near the old chapel. It was a small, one-room stone building, with two rows of pews and an altar up front. The ceiling was high and vaulted with wooden beams, and stained glass windows cast multi-colored splashes across the interior. Outside, vines crept along the old stone walls. In front of the building was a garden area, with flower bushes and benches. I didn't want to be found, so I gave the bench a miss and pushed straight into the foliage, finding a comfortable spot to sit against an old oak tree with a thick trunk. I took a deep breath, inhaling the scent of autumn leaves.

What had just happened? Some crazy guy and an awkward conversation, that's all. It was probably some lame pickup line, a way to get into my head. Maybe it was common in Iceland. If so, I should feel flattered.

It's not like he wasn't handsome. I could appreciate his perfect features, his flawless, creamy skin, his tall, lithe body with a swimmer's torso. I shook my head and steadied myself. He was the type of guy I would have been happy to appreciate from afar. But when he got up in my space like that—I've never been that close to a boy before. At least not a boy *like that.*

I'd made out with a few guys, at parties, but they were always insecure and clumsy. Too much tongue, ramming into my teeth; or sloppy drool-filled kisses that made me want to take a shower. This was different. Nobody had ever made me feel... like this. When Sebastian looked at me it felt like I had a spotlight on me, and I was melting. Which is kind of funny because I usually do fine on stage, under a spotlight... at least when I'm singing. But then I don't have to make eye contact with anyone.

I shook my head to clear my thoughts. My parents *just* died, it was my second day of school in a new country, for heaven's sake. How could I be attracting this much drama into my life when all I wanted to do was blend in and try to be normal?

But those green eyes...

I heard footsteps and made myself even smaller, hoping they'd walk past me. My heart beat faster when the footsteps stopped in front of me, but then the person sat down on the bench, and I could see his face. *Ethan.* He had his jacket off, his shirt open at the top and his tie loose. He rolled up his sleeves to the elbow, exposing muscular forearms with even more tattoos. The bell rang for the next class. Ethan didn't even flinch. I was going to be late, and now I was stuck. *Shit!* I didn't relish the thought of me stumbling out of the bushes in front of him.

He flipped his long hair out of his face, then bent down to pick up an orange oak leaf. He put the leaf on the tip of his index finger, holding the stem with his other hand. Then very slowly, he let go of the stem and balanced the leaf on his finger. That's when things started getting weird. Ethan hunched his shoulders and drew his eyebrows together in concentration, without disturbing the leaf—it looked like it was glued to the end of his finger.

Then the leaf starting spinning, slowly at first, then faster. Eyes wide, I stood up slowly to get a better look. After that, I swear the leaf jumped up and landed on his finger again, standing straight up from the stem. So now it was balanced in a physics-defying stance, like a little ballerina up on one toe, spinning on Ethan's index finger.

The branch I was leaning on broke with a loud crack. I spilled sideways, my knees sinking into the dirt. Before I could collect myself with dignity, Ethan burst through the bushes and was leaning over me with his fists clenched together.

"You again," he snarled. "Why can't you leave me alone?"

"I came out here first, long before you showed up. I had no idea you were going to be here." I stood and brushed myself off.

His eyes narrowed. "You were hiding. Spying on me," he said.

"I may have been hiding, but I wasn't spying," I said, holding his gaze.

"Did someone send you? One of the families?"

"What families?" I asked. *Why wasn't anybody making sense today?* "Believe me, I have no interest in what you do with your free time. I came out for some fresh air, then when you sat down I got stuck, I didn't want to disturb you, so I stayed hidden."

He rubbed his jaw. We were all alone, during class. And I was pretty sure I'd just seen something I wasn't supposed to. The smart thing to do would be to leave, now.

"How did you do that?" I blurted instead.

Ethan brushed his hair out of his eyes and then rolled his sleeves back down, covering the tattoos. "I don't know what you are talking about," he said finally.

"With the leaf—balancing it like that, I've never seen anything like it."

Ethan leaned in closer, until I could see the details in his amber eyes.

"I get it," he said, "You're infatuated with me. You can't help it. You're new here and trying to make friends. Maybe you think making up crazy rumors about me is going to get people to like you. But that isn't going to work for me. So get your shit together, and *get lost.*"

His words hit me like a slap in the face, and I stood frozen as he turned and walked away. *Why did he have to be such a jerk?* But I knew what I'd seen. Something about Ethan wasn't normal, and I was going to find out what.

I didn't see how the day could get any worse. I was actually looking forward to gym class, if only to focus on something simple and stop my racing mind. I grabbed the duffel bag from my locker and headed to the volleyball court, but nobody was there. I walked back to the office to ask Mrs. Weavers where I should be.

"Oh, they're at the pool today, hon," she said, wiping her glasses.

The pool?

My whole body froze.

She asked another student to show me the way to the pool building, where I met up with my class and teacher. The other students were already swimming laps.

"You must be Clara," a young woman approached me, "I'm Miss Baxter, the swimming coach. I was wondering where you'd gotten off to."

"I didn't know swimming was part of the curriculum here."

"Every Tuesday. I've got some extra suits, I'm sure one will fit you for today."

I looked down at my feet and said quietly, "I can't swim."

"You can't, eh? Is it your special friend?"

"What? No! I just—we lived in Arizona. It's dry. There was never any reason to learn."

"How interesting! We'll, you can just practice in the shallow end. Maybe I can give you some after school lessons. Swimming isn't that hard."

My body was going into panic mode. I felt the adrenaline kick in and my brow start to sweat. This was how I felt whenever I had to stand in front of the class and give a presentation. But my fear of public speaking couldn't compare to my lifelong terror of the water, ever since that day at the beach in Oregon.

I shook my head and bit my lip, not sure how to explain.

"I have aquaphobia," I said. "Persistent and abnormal fear of water."

She gave me a funny look, and I knew she thought I was making it up, and considering whether to force me in the water or send me to the principal's office.

My eyes welled up and my lip started quivering.

I'm not going to cry. Not going to—

I felt so stupid, but today had already been confusing and emotional, with the unexpected confrontations with both Sebastian and Ethan. The idea of learning to swim in the shallow end in front of Brianna and Roisin, like a baby, mortified me.

I squeezed my eyes shut but tears were already spilling past the walled gates of my eyelids.

Stop it! You're embarrassing yourself.

By now the whole class had stopped swimming and was watching us. I could see Roisin smirk and I knew the whole school was going to hear about this. I couldn't take it anymore. I ran out of the pool area before Miss Baxter could decide what to do with me.

Not sure where to go, I ended up at my locker.

There was a large piece of notebook paper taped to it.

Go home, Yankee.

It was too much. I sank to the ground with my back against my locker, letting the tears stream down my face. I obviously wasn't wanted here.

9

I blew Jackie and Derry off after school. The long bus ride home was painful, as Jackie tried to figure out what was wrong and I just retreated further into myself. Then I rushed home and tore off my uniform. The black leather dress shoes felt like they were sucking out my soul. I put on sweats and a T-shirt. When Aedan got home I told him I felt sick and didn't want to go to school the next day.

I could tell he didn't believe me, but he let it slide. I stayed in bed for most of the evening, catching up on all the TV shows I liked, downloading and binge watching episodes. I tried to get on Facebook and message Beth, but with the time difference she was probably sleeping.

Hate it here

Ireland sucks

Everyone hates me

Then I got on my typewriter and pounded on the keys for about an hour, until my fingertips were aching. What was it about Sebastian that made me feel so confused? What kind of kid shows up out of nowhere and goes skinny-dipping in the middle of the night? And how the hell had Ethan done that trick with the leaf? Jackie had said something about magic, but magic wasn't *real*. Whatever was going on, I wanted no part in it. They wanted me to go home? *I didn't even want to be here!*

Around 8pm, Aedan knocked on my door. When I opened it, he came in and set a tray of soup and bread on my desk.

"Feeling better?" he asked.

"No, not really," I said.

"Want to talk about it?"

I sighed. "It's stupid." I couldn't tell him what I was feeling. The self-pity and depression soaking into me, like inky tendrils sucking the happiness out of my body. I couldn't stop thinking about that nasty note: the second I'd received in less than a week since arrival. With all the other stuff going on, it was just so cruel. What kind of person is mean to a girl who just buried her parents?

"Now I doubt that," Aedan said. "You're dealing with things... nobody as young as you should have to."

That made me feel even worse. I *should* be upset about my parents. Instead I was freaking out about being embarrassed in front of my classmates. *I am so messed up.* I was ashamed to confess I was just being teased, or having boy trouble.

"I was afraid school might be too much, too soon. Overwhelming."

"It's not school. It's just, I don't belong here. I don't fit in. Nobody likes me."

"It takes time to make new friends, but I don't believe for a second that nobody likes you. You're a kind, smart girl. When life gives you challenges, running away is rarely the solution. You've got to face your problems so you can get through them. Otherwise they'll just stick with you and fester."

I scowled at Aedan's fortune-cookie advice. He was treating me like a normal teenage girl, but I wasn't just dealing with normal teenage problems. He had no idea what I was going through. "This isn't my life," I snapped at him. "I left my life behind in America."

"But, you're here now..."

"Don't you get it? I don't belong here. Everything I've ever cared about—all my dreams and plans, gone. I don't even know who I am anymore!"

A flash of sadness came over his face, and for a second he looked very old, and very tired.

"You're so much like your mother," he hung his head. I felt bad for yelling at him.

"Look, I know you're just trying to help, but I really need to be alone right now," I said. "I promise I'll be fine. I just need a day off. Cool?"

"Cool," he said, with a slight grin that didn't remove the worry from his eyes. "No school tomorrow. But from next week, I'll expect better attendance."

***

I refused to get out of bed the next morning. I stayed under the blankets reading fantasy novels until the early afternoon. Around 1pm I got a text from Jackie.

You OK?

I'm fine. Just didn't feel like coming to school

At home?

Yeah

Be there in 30 minutes

Crap. I wasn't ready to see people. I'd spent the day wallowing in self-pity. I dragged myself out of bed, and realized I hadn't taken a shower for almost two days. I smelled my armpits to check. *Yuck.* I wrinkled my nose. I took a quick shower. The doorbell rang as I was scrubbing my skin.

"Just a minute," I yelled, not sure if anybody could hear me.

I checked the clock by my bed and thought about getting dressed, but didn't want to leave Jackie waiting outside, so I answered the door wearing a towel and dripping on the floor.

Blond hair and green eyes met me. *Holy Shit.*

Sebastian was standing outside wearing crisp khaki pants and a pink V-neck t-shirt; he looked like he belonged in a Banana Republic summer catalogue. Totally out of place, and yet, everything around him seemed to frame him, supporting his good looks. He was a thing of beauty.

"Sorry to... interrupt," said Sebastian, raising one eyebrow at my towel-clad torso.

"What are you doing here?" I practically spat.

"Can I come in?" he asked, looking over my shoulder.

Shit shit shit. I was acutely aware of how little space was between us—or how little clothing for that matter. And I didn't think Aedan would want me entertaining guys while he was at work.

"Um, nobody's home right now. Can you... wait outside for a minute?"

I closed the door before I could change my mind, or before he could argue. I felt a little bit of satisfaction making him wait. I dashed to my bedroom and threw on a pair of jeans. I grabbed the nicest top I had—the blue one my mom always said brought out my eyes—but decided it was too formal, so I pulled on the largest sweater I owned over it. It fit like a pillowcase. I laced up my blue Docs and brushed my hair quickly.

When I opened the door for the second time, Jackie was just arriving with Derry in tow.

"Hi!" she said, giving me a hug.

"Why aren't you guys in school?" I asked.

"Playing hookie, to check up on you," Derry said. "Seems like we're not the only ones with that idea." He nodded at Sebastian.

"I was worried about her," Sebastian said, but a little less confidently than I was used to seeing him. Apparently he wasn't expecting a crowd. But he rebounded quickly.

"Since we're all here—how about that tour you promised?" he nudged Jackie.

"Oh that's a great idea. I was thinking coffee, or maybe Portrush, we have all day. And we need to make plans for your birthday dinner!" she said.

I groaned, "How'd you know?"

"Aedan called me last night," she said. "Asked me to organize something and invite some friends." *Of course he did.* He's worried about me, after I blew up at him.

"It's your birthday?" Sebastian said. He looked worried, almost afraid.

"Sweet sixteen," Derry said. "Though the dinner was supposed to be a surprise." He frowned at Jackie.

"Aedan wanted to take us out to a nice restaurant. I told him we'd rather cook ourselves, so we can drink, but we agreed to let you have the final say."

Derry had been eyeing Sebastian strangely, and I realized he wasn't sure whether or not to invite him. I thought about it. I couldn't deny I was curious about him. And he'd come to my house looking for me; maybe he needed to talk to me about something important. Maybe, I thought with a start, he even had some of the answers I was looking for.

"You can come, too—if you want," I said.

"If you're sure I'd be welcome," he said, with a smile that made my knees go weak.

"I don't really have any other friends," I said. "It wouldn't be much of a party without more guests."

"So we're friends now, are we?" A playful spark danced in his eyes.

"As long as you get me a big present," I joked. For a minute I was afraid my humor wouldn't translate well, but everybody laughed.

It was a bright, clear day, and being outside during school hours, with the sun shining and the blue sea on the horizon, it was hard not to be happy. I thought about Aedan, and the fight we'd had yesterday. I was being childish, and he was right, I couldn't just hide out in my room forever. So I'd made some enemies already. So what? *That's high school.* At least I'd also made some friends.

"Dinner at home sounds great," I said. "We can bring groceries home in the afternoon?"

"Perfect," Jackie said.

Derry had brought his car—a black Volkswagen Golf. The boys took the front seats while Jackie and I squeezed into the back. I told them I'd already seen Dunluce Castle. I wouldn't mind going back to see it again, but they wanted to show me something new. We decided to go to Giant's Causeway, the other major attraction nearby. After a few minutes driving along the coastal highway, Sebastian pointed to a small exit ahead.

"Derry, would you mind turning left here?" he asked.

"You want to see the Runkerry House?"

"Something like that," Sebastian said with a grin.

We pulled up outside an old manor house, right on the edge of a bluff looking over the sea. It was enormous. It looked like a university, with sprawling brick buildings, wrought iron gates, and gray rooftops with about a dozen chimneys poking up. The front yard was filled with wild grass and wildflowers.

Sebastian got out and took a set of keys from his pockets.

"Shut up!" Jackie said, her eyes wide. "You *live* here?"

"For the moment." Sebastian unlocked the heavy iron gates so that Derry could drive through. Jackie and I got out also, while Derry parked the car.

"This place is incredible," Jackie said as we climbed the stairs. Sebastian opened the front door and we walked into a wide foyer with high ceilings, illuminated by large sea-facing windows. On the walls were oil paintings in heavy gilded frames, and the furniture looked antique, but tasteful. I caught a glimpse of a study, with a wide oak desk and a floor to ceiling bookshelf. Derry whistled when Sebastian opened the door to his apartment.

Although the entrance had an old-fashioned, classical European feel, with decorative moldings and pillars, the inner apartment was clean and modern. The walls and ceiling were white. Wide silver couches split up the living room, and the large windows allowed an uninterrupted view of the sea. One corner of the apartment was made entirely of glass, with a comfortable reading nook in the corner. There was a marble fireplace carved with flourishes, pots with fresh flowers, hanging chandeliers and a few old leather chairs I wanted to sink into.

"I've lived here my whole life and never been inside. It's not even open for tours. I didn't know it was for sale," Derry said.

"I didn't buy it," Sebastian said. "I'm just leasing it temporarily."

"You mean your parents are leasing it," I prompted. Sebastian avoided my question.

In the center of the room was a massive dining table, made from a solid piece of wood with eight chairs around it. In one corner was a small kitchen, and there were benches and small tables near the windows. The room opened onto a balcony, with more furniture – low white couches and swinging chairs, even a hammock.

"Who are you? Some famous actor's secret son?" Jackie teased.

"Actually... my parents aren't in town with me at the moment," Sebastian said.

Alarm bells were going off in my head. He showed up in town, alone, and has enough money to rent this huge place by himself?

"Lucky you," Derry said. "I wish I could live on my own."

"Isn't this place a little... excessive?" Jackie said, looking around. "Three bedrooms, right? Just for you?"

"I wanted somewhere with a lot of privacy. The owner lives abroad and the agent said I could rent it indefinitely for only 5,000 euro a month."

He said it like he'd gotten a bargain, like 5,000 euro wasn't a small fortune. Most college kids at home couldn't afford to afford to pay a tenth of that on rent.

"But... where'd you get the money?" I asked.

"My father is a... he works for the military," Sebastian said with a shrug.

Iceland has a military?

"Do you know the history of this place?" Jackie asked Derry.

"I'm a tour guide in the summer," Derry explained. "But like I said, I've never been in here. I think it was built in the early 1860s. It was used by the Northern Ireland government, then converted to a retirement home. There was a controversy when it was sold; something about the moral rights of the government to sell a charitably donated property. Last I heard they were going to convert it to a 5 Star Hotel or golf club. Funded by Donald Trump."

The pounding surf drew me closer to the windows. All you could see was dark blue water, and the light blue sky. Then I saw my own reflection in the glass: my skinny black jeans and baggy gray sweater, my dark hair. I saw another face in the glass and turned around to catch Sebastian staring.

He looked down quickly and went into the bedroom. I gave Jackie a look. *Was he just looking at my ass?* She smirked but didn't say anything. When Sebastian came back I saw him stuff something white in his pocket. "I just needed to pick something up," he said. "Should we go?"

"Do we have to?" Derry replied, sinking into a leather bean bag chair in the all glass reading nook. Even that section of the floor was glass. A narrow strip had been cut into the rocks, leading to a manmade pool directly under the building. It was about a foot deep and filled with fish and sea creatures.

"You could have your party here, if you want..." Sebastian offered. Derry looked hopeful, but I didn't think Aedan would be comfortable coming over. Plus he'd find out that Sebastian lived alone. I shook my head.

"Another time, then." Sebastian gestured to the door.

"Another time, *please*," Derry said.

As we were leaving I felt my shoes crunch on something. I bent down, thinking it might be broken glass. I picked up a few grains and rubbed them between my fingers. *Sand.*

"You need a housekeeper," Jackie said.

"I have one," Sebastian smiled but it didn't reach his eyes. Instead he looked nervous. "She must have missed that. I walk on the beach a lot."

Back on the road, we saw Giant's Causeway as we rounded the next bend in the seashore. I gasped—the volcanic rock formations of were much larger and more dramatic than I'd pictured.

"Over 40,000 interlocking hexagonal blocks of stone," Derry said, going into his tour guide spiel. "Local legend says that Fionn Mac Cumhaill built it so he could battle Benandonner, his rival across the strait in Scotland."

"Go on," Sebastian said, "I'd love to hear the rest of the story."

"Well... when Benandonner showed up for the big fight," Derry continued, "Fionn was startled as he spied the Scottish giant's bulk. So he asked his wife, Oonagh, to disguise him as a baby. She put him in an outsized baby's crib, and covered him with a blanket."

We parked the car and started walking towards the stones.

"Oonagh told Benandonner that Fionn was out hunting and would return soon. She asked him to wait nearby as she fed their baby. As soon as Benandonner saw the size of the "infant," he assumed that its father, Fionn, must be a giant among giants. So he turned around and fled back to Scotland in terror, destroying the Causeway behind him in case Fionn wanted to follow."

"That's one story," Jackie said, lightly hopping up the stones, one by one. "Other people call them the stepping stones of the Fomori."

Sebastian blanched at this, but kept silent.

"Fomori?" I asked.

"From the old Irish, *muire*, or *sea*," Derry said. "Legendary beings from under the sea. Mythological creatures of chaos and violence."

Sebastian snorted and his eyes darkened.

"But really it's just a natural volcanic formation," Derry finished lamely.

"That's natural?" I asked, incredulous that nature could churn out so many six sided columns of stone, locked together like puzzle pieces, with perfectly flat tops.

"In the 1840s, tourists would hire local boatmen on the beach. To properly see the columns of the Causeway they would plough through the breakers and then row back into the bay for the best view of the Causeway and the nearby shore caves. In 1897 a company won a court case to fence the stones off and charge admission," Derry recited.

The boys started jumping across the rocks, trying to balance on the highest columns of stone. Jackie and I lagged behind, and then found a spot to sit, marveling at the alien landscape.

"So what's up with you and Sebastian?" she asked, taking her sunglasses off and putting them up on top of her head.

"What? Nothing," I said.

"You didn't invite him over to your house?" she asked.

"No, he just showed up…" I suddenly wondered how he knew where I lived.

Jackie shrugged, "He likes you."

I looked at Jackie. She was wearing cute jean shorts, and tied her shirt at her waist showing off her belly button. Her hair glowed like fire in the afternoon sun, and I could see that she had very faint freckles. *If he likes me, instead of Jackie, there must be something wrong with him.* But he did show up at my house today. Could Jackie be right? Or was there another reason he kept showing up?

"I don't know," I said finally. "He's pretty intense."

"And hot," Jackie said. "He can't take his eyes off of you." She nodded, and sure enough, Sebastian was up ahead, watching us, as if he were listening. He bent down to pick something up, pretending to ignore us. He held it up to his nose and smelled it.

"He's a little weird though," Jackie said, wrinkling her nose.

"You noticed that?" I laughed.

I couldn't deny Sebastian was gorgeous. But why would a guy like that be interested in me?

"I just—I don't know what he wants from me."

Jackie gave me a knowing look and pinched my cheek.

"I'm sure boys in America aren't all that different from boys here," she said. "They just want some attention for their wee baldy fella."

I blushed at the euphemism, and shoved her a little.

"I'm not... ready to be involved with anyone."

She put her arm around my shoulder and gave me a squeeze.

"Or, a good ride might be just what you need. Don't wait too long though."

"Why not?"

"Because if he flirts with me, even a little bit, I'm totally going to jump him. And I'll never give him back."

"I thought you and Derry..."

"Uh, no. He's great, but we're just friends. He's more my older brother. Besides, I'm not sure whether I'm his cup of tea," she said with a wink.

"He's gay?" I said, reading her meaning.

"He's never said anything to me about it. Maybe he's just really shy around girls. Let's just say it's an intuition I have about him, that might be misplaced. Don't say anything though."

"Lips sealed," I promised.

We explored the coastline and the strange formations until the sun started going down. As I watched the sky turn pink and orange, and the sinking sun's reflection over the ocean, Sebastian came up and stood next to me. There was a gust of wind, and his hand brushed against mine. I felt a tingling spread over my skin, and shivered. But then I crossed my arms. I wasn't ready to swoon just yet.

"What did you mean before, at school," I said. "Something about *my kind.*"

"Nothing, never mind. I … I made a mistake."

I frowned and glared up at him.

"It's just something we say in Iceland to pretty girls," he said.

Did he just call me pretty?

I blushed, even though I was trying to control myself. There were a million reasons why romance shouldn't be on my to do list. And besides, didn't they say that grief made you horny? I couldn't trust my body right now. But I was in this amazingly unreal landscape, at sunset, standing next to an epically handsome guy who for some reason kept hanging around me. A small part of me felt like a princess in a fantasy. I licked my lips, thinking that the romance would be heightened if he decided to grab me and kiss me like the world was ending. Then I chased the image out of my head. *What's wrong with me?*

Maybe Jackie was right. I was almost sixteen, and for some reason, this hot guy seemed interested in me. He thought I was cute. What else could it be? Even though I'd given him no encouragement and had no idea how to flirt, here he was watching the sunset with me.

Since I got to Ireland I'd become obsessed with finding out more about my mother, even imagining that I was in danger. But maybe my mother's problems were *her* problems. Maybe I'd never discover her reasons for leaving Ireland, or what really happened to Colin, or for lying to me. Aedan was right, I shouldn't shut the world out. This was my life now. I wasn't going back to America any time soon. I might as well make the best of it, and maybe Sebastian was my chance. If he was hiding something from me, and I'm not sure he was, he probably had good reasons for it. And I'm not sure I wanted to know.

10

It started out as the perfect birthday party, and ended with a dead girl. I was still on an emotional high from the day at the beach, and every time Sebastian looked my way I felt butterflies in my stomach. Jackie thought he liked me. And why else would he show up at my house, or hang out with us all day long, and then come back to Aedan's house for dinner? It's like he had nowhere else he wanted to be. The constant dull ache in my heart since my parents' death was starting to loosen up, and instead of feeling guilty about that, I felt relieved. I knew my parents wouldn't want me to be morose. I was glad to be feeling happy for a change. Of course the two glasses of wine probably had something to do with my sudden optimism.

Derry was telling a funny story and I laughed out loud, snorting into my wine glass. Aedan watched me curiously, probably counting the cups of wine I drank. I'm sure he would have cut me off after the first one if it weren't my birthday.

Sebastian smiled politely but never really relaxed. But it was my party. I could laugh if I wanted to. For just one day, I was going to pretend to be a normal, happy, teenage girl.

Aedan had made pasta with chunky vegetables in the sauce, and the kitchen still smelled like rosemary and oregano. Aedan went into the living room and returned with a deck of cards, with Miscreant weaving between his legs. "Fancy a game of 25's?"

Sebastian nodded, "It's been awhile but I'm sure it'll come back to me."

"I've never actually played," Jackie said.

"I learned once but I forget," Derry said. "How's it go: *Five, Jack, Ace of Hearts, Ace of Trumps, Royals, Highest in Red, Lowest in Black?* Something about robbing and reneging?"

It took a few rounds before I got the hang of it, and then I held my own. When I finally reached twenty-five points and won a round, Aedan decided it was a good place to stop. He went into the kitchen and brought out an upside down applesauce cake with walnuts and white frosting, and a single lit candle sticking out of it.

"Happy birthday to you..." Aedan started, and the others joined in, clapping their hands. I honestly didn't know what to wish for. For the last four years I'd wished to become a professional singer. That goal seemed far away now, though I hadn't given up on it. And wishing for it again, when I had so little control over my future, seemed scarier, like I'd jinx it somehow. And I couldn't handle thinking about it. If I wasn't a singer, what else could I do with my life? I had no idea, and the enormity of my ignorance threatened to break down the walls of sanity I'd been trying to hold up over the last few weeks. So I decided to keep it simple.

What else did I want? I glanced up at Sebastian, and he smiled at me. I was grinning so hard when I blew out my candle, I had to bite my lip to stop. After we'd had cake, it was getting stuffy in the small house, so we went outside for some air. Derry lit a cigarette and shared it with Jackie. The coastal air was fresh and a little biting. A sudden gust of wind took my breath away and I shivered. Sebastian took off his jacket and wrapped it around my shoulders. I suddenly felt warmed up, from the inside out. Jackie raised an eyebrow at me, then grabbed Derry's arm.

"We're going back inside, but you guys take your time," she said, pulling him into the house.

Sebastian made no move to leave. I could feel his body next to mine, my right hand just inches from his left, as we turned together and looked out over the sea. It was almost black now, the horizon marked only by the beginning of the starry sky. The moon had been full a few nights ago, now it was waning. I put my hands in the pockets of Sebastian's coat, and my fingertips brushed against something. I pulled it out—a shiny piece of blue ribbon.

"What's this?" I asked.

"Nothing," he shrugged. "Saw it at the beach today, picked it up. I hate seeing trash near the ocean."

Handsome and eco-friendly. I wanted to make a smart comment, but I couldn't think of any, so I stayed quiet, listening to the waves. My heart was pounding in my ears. The air between us was thick, and seemed charged with energy. I wondered if I should grab his hand, or lean onto his shoulder. Maybe he was too shy to make the first move—though that seemed unlikely.

"Close your eyes," he said after a few moments, reaching into his pocket. He lifted the corners of his mouth, but the gesture didn't reach his eyes.

"Why?" I asked. My heart fluttered and my palms were sweating. I remembered the note on my doorstep, and the missing girl. Was it stupid to be alone with him in the dark? What if he's reaching for a weapon? He could totally be a serial killer. I didn't know anything about this guy: where he came from, or why he showed up mysteriously just a few days after I did.

Sebastian lifted his fingertips to my eyebrows and very slowly let them fall, brushing my eyelids shut. My insides turned to butter. I kept my eyes closed, and licked my lips. I felt tremendously excited—and a little nervous—for the kiss I was sure was coming.

I held my breath as he moved behind me and lifted up my hair. I felt something cold against my neck, and his fingertips brushed against my collarbone.

"Like it?" he said in a low voice behind me. I could feel his breath against my cheek.

I opened my eyes, and reached up to feel the delicate string of beads around my neck. No, not beads. *Pearls.*

"You look beautiful," he said. He stood in front of me, looking straight into my eyes, and for the first time, I didn't run away or duck my chin.

He reached up and tucked a strand of hair behind my ear.

The wine made me bold. And it was my birthday, and a handsome guy just gave me pearls. I felt like I was in some romantic movie, and I knew what came next.

I leaned into him, tilting my lips up towards his. I closed my eyes, waiting for him to close the gap between us, to feel the brush of his lips on mine...

Instead I felt him shudder, and then turn away.

The rejection felt like an ice pick into my heart.

First I was embarrassed, thinking I must have misread the situation. But I thought the pearls had been a pretty clear message; why would he give me a gift like that if he didn't want to kiss me? If he didn't like me, what was he even doing here?

The tension between our bodies was unbearable.

"Sorry—" I stumbled, "I thought you wanted..." I left the sentence unfinished, feeling confused and hurt.

"It's not you," he said, frowning.

"Sure. I shouldn't have, anyway. I'm a little drunk. Forget it ever happened. I should go."

I felt nauseous. The alcohol had clouded my judgment and I'd made a fool of myself. I needed to get away from him until I could think clearly. I turned towards the house abruptly.

He grabbed my wrist, and spun me back around, then took my shoulders with both hands. His eyes were the greenest I'd ever seen them.

"I want to. Believe me I want to," he said.

"Forget it. It's fine," I lied.

"It's just—I can't. It's... *forbidden.*"

His words hit me like a bucket of ice.

What!?

Suddenly I was angry.

"Look I don't care if you don't want to kiss me," I said. "I'm not your type, or you don't like me that way, or whatever. I'll deal with it. But don't make up some bullshit excuse."

I was almost shaking with rage when I ran into the house and slammed the door. And that's when I saw the dead girl. Aedan had turned on the news, and everybody was standing around the TV. Jackie had one hand to her mouth, and the expression on her face froze me in my tracks.

On screen was a view of Giant's Causeway, where we'd been standing just hours ago. The caption read, *missing girl found dead on beach*. A reporter was interviewing a fat woman with a little white dog.

"So I was just taking Brighton here for a walk, and I saw someone lying on the rocks, which isn't all that weird, but she was surrounded by flowers. I thought they were filming a movie or something, but it was just her, so I went to see what was going on. The most bizarre thing, she's laid out in a pretty blue dress, a ring of flowers around her, her hands folded neatly on her stomach, as pretty as you please, and ribbons in her hair."

I looked over at Sebastian, and what I saw gave me chills. While the rest of us looked surprised or shocked, he hardly flinched. If anything, he looked *guilty*. I reached into my pocket and fingered the blue ribbon, the one Sebastian said he'd found on the beach. My gut twisted and I *knew*, somehow, that it belonged to Bedelia Meath.

***

When Aedan found out that we'd already known about the missing girl, I thought he was going to yell at me. Instead he said quietly, "I think it's time for your friends to go home." I could tell Sebastian wanted to stay and talk. His eyes seemed to be pleading with me. *Give me a chance to explain.* But Aedan shooed them out. After they left he gave me a lecture about responsibility, and made me promise I wouldn't go anywhere alone and that I'd keep my cell phone on all the time.

Alone in my bedroom, I tried to get a handle on my raging emotions. My fingers against the typewriter didn't bring the comfort I was looking for. Did I really suspect Sebastian of killing Bedelia? He was strange, but he didn't seem like a psychopath. But what did I really know about him? Had he really found the ribbon on the beach, or was it a keepsake from his latest victim? But if that were true, why would he agree to come to Giant's Causeway at all? Wouldn't he recommend somewhere else?

These questions helped keep my mind off the other thing I'd found out tonight, the thing that was squeezing the air out of my lungs, making me gasp for air. The thing that had shattered my heart. *He doesn't want me.* I hated that the rejection meant so much to me. I barely knew Sebastian, and until the moment he pulled away, I wasn't even sure that I liked him. I'd let Jackie convince me that there was something between us, and I'd been dreaming of a fantasy romance where none existed. I tried to distract myself with homework or Facebook for a while, but I couldn't shake the emptiness in my chest, a void so empty and aching it was almost painful. Then I got a text from Jackie.

What happened with Sebastian?
You looked upset when you came inside
Did he try something?

I wish. I thought.
I was crying because... he gave me pearls?
How could I explain that?

I thought he wanted to kiss me...

I touched the pearls around my neck again, remembering his fingertips on my collarbone.

But then, he didn't.

Thinking about Sebastian brought warmth to my body. *What's wrong with me?* How could I be thinking about boys when they'd just found Bedelia? If anything, I wanted Sebastian to kiss me even more. *I'm disgusting.* Maybe her death had just reminded me of how short and tragic life was. Some people say death is an aphrodisiac, right?

I thought leaving America behind, I'd somehow closed the door on loss and death, and gone through a reality portal; I'd thought somehow Ireland would be green hills and flowers and a fresh start. But death had followed me.

I couldn't believe how melodramatic I was becoming. The typewriter allowed me the freedom to explore my darkest thoughts, without worrying about them being accidentally discovered. A ding alerted me to a new message from Jackie.

That's nothing, he probably chickened out

He's obviously into you, there must just be something holding him back. Maybe he just broke up with someone... give him time

I wanted to believe her, but there was something about the way Sebastian pulled away from me... like he physically couldn't stand to be near me. Almost like he found me repulsive. *What was that about?*

And even though I'd never met her, I couldn't get Bedelia out of my mind. It was weird that she turned up in the same place we'd just been, but that had to be a coincidence. *Another* coincidence. I was probably fixating morosely, that's what a psychologist would have said. If I were being honest with myself, the knot in my stomach probably had more to do with seeing Sebastian at school the next day, and wondering if he'd ignore me or avoid me now. *Whatever.* I had more important things to think about. And I was going back to the states in a couple years for school anyway. It could never have worked between us.

I took the pearls off and set them on my desk. Maybe Jackie was right; maybe Sebastian just chickened out. Why would he give me a gift like that if he didn't like me? I still felt like a fool, throwing myself at a guy I'd only known for a few days. But I'd been entirely too distracted by boys recently. Tomorrow I'd be sixteen. I had two more years before I graduated, and I needed to focus on school if I wanted to get into a top opera program. Though I went to sleep with a heavy heart.

That night I dreamed I was up on the cliff again.

It was so vivid, I could hear the wind in my ears. Feel the cool, fresh grass between my toes.

Sebastian was behind me, holding me. He wrapped his arms around me and I could feel his body pressing against mine. And then we were surrounded by water. Floating, sinking. I could feel the throbbing of the ocean and it matched my heartbeat, each wave pounding against the shore reverberated through my body like a gong. I should have been terrified, but for some reason, I wasn't. I felt warm and secure, safe. Protected.

Then there was a blinding light.

11

I woke up with a headache, clutching the piece of blue ribbon, and hating myself as the confusing jumble of memories from last night hit my brain. *Did I really yell at Sebastian for not kissing me?*

I rolled out of bed, my fingers itching to touch the cool keys of my typewriter. I didn't care how early it was, I needed to process. I remembered my dream about Sebastian, and typed out my thoughts, imagining them appear on an invisible piece of paper.

When I went into the living room, I found Aedan asleep in his arm chair with an empty bottle of wine next to him. He must have stayed up late, drinking by himself. Then I saw the note in his lap.

I recognized my mother's handwriting, and reached for the note, carefully slipping the paper from Aedan's fingers.

I love you, Dad, but I can't live here in this small town anymore. I need to find myself, somewhere new where nobody knows my past. I'm sorry I can't explain more in person or justify this choice. It tears me apart to be the second woman to leave you, but know that I wouldn't if it weren't absolutely necessary. Trust me that it's for the best. Yours, forever, Branna.

I assumed the first woman to leave must have been my grandmother. I didn't want to be another woman who left him, and hoped I wouldn't have to. The note didn't say anything about Colin. Was it possible that she'd left town, and then someone had killed him later on the same day? I put the note back, careful not to disturb him, though I was tempted to wake him up and ask questions. *Where did my grandma come from? Why did she leave?*

I was certain he knew more than he was telling me, but I didn't feel comfortable enough with Aedan yet to ask. He was obviously still hurting, even after all these years. The news of a murderer who was targeting young girls couldn't have helped.

I put a blanket over him and got ready for school.

I got dressed and then started brushing my hair in the bathroom. The brush clattered in the sink when I saw my mother's face staring back at me from the mirror with a surprised expression.

I rubbed my eyes.

What the hell?

I waved my hand. So did the reflection.

I turned my head, and my mother's doppelganger followed.

It was definitely me in the mirror. But everything was slightly different. *Better.* The changes were subtle. If I weren't examining myself closely, I might have missed them.

My hair was darker, and silky smooth. I shook my hands through it and watched the sheen glide flawlessly down to its tips. I looked like a shampoo commercial. Guess I wouldn't need to spend ten minutes brushing the knots out of my hair this morning.

My nose, which had always been a tiny bit too round and bulbous—looked straighter, the edges more defined. My lips were full and red, like I'd been chewing on them. Even my breasts felt swollen, leaving an appreciable amount of smooth cleavage, the curves of which bounced in the light as I moved my arms. My skin was flawless, like I had a layer of foundation on, and my dark eyebrows arched gracefully towards my ears. As I was admiring them, the left eyebrow jumped up quizzically and I covered my mouth with my hand in surprise.

I'd always been jealous of people who could raise one eyebrow, because I'd never been able to do it before. Suddenly it seemed like second nature. I practiced raising one, and then the other, until they were dancing—and then laughed out loud.

But the most noticeable thing were my eyes. They'd always been a murky blue-gray, a hue that seemed to shift a bit with the weather and my clothes. Now they were a soft teal, like glacier water, the edges lined with a rim of darker blue. I was still me, but I looked like I'd had a professional makeover for the cover of Seventeen Magazine. And then been Photoshopped to perfection.

Is this how I'm going to look when I roll out of bed from now on? I wondered if anybody else would notice. Maybe it was all in my head. Maybe it was the lighting in the bathroom, or my subconscious telling me I was a year older and altering my self-perception.

I got dressed and grabbed an apple off the kitchen table, before walking to the bus stop. Finally I saw Jackie approaching. She did a double take when she saw me, then grabbed my chin and turned it from side to side.

"Nicely done," she said. *She thinks I did this?* "The lads are going to eat you up."

Only one crossed my mind.

***

I'd always been jealous of my mother's looks: the way men would turn their head to look at her. Not that it did any favors for my self-esteem. People used to wonder whether I was adopted. They couldn't believe such a plain little girl could come from such a glamorous woman. We had some similar features, and I wasn't ugly – but standing next to my mother I was invisible. I'd gotten used to flying under the radar.

Until today. Now, it was like a cameraman was following me around. Guys rubbernecked as I walked past, or even stopped in their tracks to ogle. In first period I finally let Patricia do my wardrobe makeover, pinning my skirt a few inches above my knees. When she'd finished, she leaned back in her chair and nodded in approval.

"It's insane how hot you look right now," she said. "Lucky we're friends already or I'd be tempted to hate you."

"Don't worry, I'm still socially awkward."

"Yes, there is that." She smirked.

She wasn't the only one paying attention. I'm pretty sure I saw Mr. Halpern fixating on my thighs and then looking guilty about it during History class. *This is not good.* I never had guys stare at me like this before. Luckily I wasn't the only topic of conversation—after all, there was a dead girl to talk about. I'd been hearing snippets of conversation and gossip about Bedelia all day. The way she was found, presented like an offering, suggested foul-play.

On the bus this morning Derry, Jackie and I had gotten our stories straight. Of course we hadn't done anything wrong, but neither were we eager to tell everybody that we'd skipped school to hang out at Giant's Causeway the same day a girl's body was discovered. Or that we'd been celebrating my birthday when we first saw the news. I hadn't wanted to be associated with Bedelia when she was *missing*. Now that she was dead, I was desperate to avoid any connection. Jackie was too mature to say *I told you so*, but I guessed she was thinking it. The note and what happened to Bedelia were probably unrelated, but now I'd never know. Could she have been saved if I'd gone to the police? Was I withholding information that lead to her death?

Most of the teachers made a small comment at the beginning of class but then went straight into the curriculum. Mr. Sadleir, however, decided to turn the event into a teachable moment.

"I know some of you were friends with Bedelia, and that even those of you who didn't know her well may be dealing with some strong emotions. First let me say that there is no 'right' way to feel about her death. Everybody mourns in a different way. If you need to cry, or talk about it, that's fine. If you need space to grieve privately, that's fine. Some people may even want to laugh or be silly. But one of the most beautiful ways to express our emotions is through writing. Yes, grief can be beautiful, as can death. Suffering, regret, tragedy—they are painful and difficult to deal with, but the ability to care enough to feel loss defines us as humans." Then he handed out a section from Hamlet, describing the death of Ophelia.

> *When down her weedy trophies and herself*
> *Fell in the weeping brook. Her clothes spread wide;*
> *And, mermaid-like, awhile they bore her up:*
> *Which time she chanted snatches of old tunes;*
> *As one incapable of her own distress,*
> *Or like a creature native and indued*
> *Unto that element: but long it could not be*
> *Till that her garments, heavy with their drink,*
> *Pull'd the poor wretch from her melodious lay*
> *To muddy death.*

A girl in the back of the room started crying and Mr. Sadleir handed her a tissue. Then he told us, if we wanted to, we could write a poem about Bedelia. We could turn it in or simply keep it to ourselves. Something about the exercise left me cold, so I cracked a book instead and caught up on our readings. The empty chair to my side taunted me. Sebastian wasn't in class. I was anxious about seeing him after what happened—or didn't happen—between us at my party. I was worried it was going to be awkward, but I wanted to see his reaction to my changed appearance. *If he liked me before, maybe he'd like me more now?*

Instead I got Travis. After class he found me in the hallway and walked with me for a while, sneaking glances at my face and asking how I'd been. I tried to be polite, but his small talk was driving me out of my mind. When he asked me whether Bedelia's death was upsetting me, because it was so soon after losing my parents, I couldn't take any more.

"I've got to run and find a friend of mine, nice chatting with you," I said, and practically ran down the hall. Jackie, Derry, Patricia and Kyle were already at our table and I slid in next to them.

"So here's the really weird thing," Derry was saying, "Normally it could be ruled an accidental drowning, or possibly a staged suicide. But the positioning of the body could only have been done *after* her death. Which meant it was probably a bizarre, ritualistic murder of some kind. A message maybe."

"Not necessarily," Patricia said. "She could have dressed up, spread the flowers, taken a few pills and just lain there until she died. It's dramatic, but it makes a statement. If I were going to commit suicide, that's how I'd want to do it."

"Firstly," Kyle said, "if you ever commit suicide, I will resuscitate your body and then kill you. Don't even joke about that. Secondly, you'd have to take a lot of OTC medication to kill yourself, and you would die in agony. It would be nearly impossible to hold a pose. But anyway, I heard the toxicology report was clean. No drugs. Because of the water in her lungs, the coroner said she died of drowning. She had help, whether she wanted it or not."

I pictured long, slender fingers holding Bedelia underwater as she opened her mouth in a silent scream. I shuddered involuntarily. Drowning like that was my worst nightmare. Which is why the dream I had last night was really weird. How could something that terrified me so much, make me feel so good?

"But who would do something like that, and why?" Derry asked.

Jackie shrugged, munching on a carrot. Kyle went to chat with some of his friends, and Patricia got up to refill her drink. When I looked up from my sandwich, Jackie and Derry were exchanging looks.

"What?" I asked.

"Well, it just seems like, maybe there's some connection, between what's going on with you…" Jackie prompted.

"And a murderer? Not likely."

"What about the note? The photograph?"

"I got a weird note on my door. I saw a guy who creeped me out a bit. But that doesn't seem to have anything to do with Bedelia. If anything it's about what happened to my mother a long time ago. Colin didn't drown, he was stabbed. Whoever did this, laying out the body like that, he obviously put a lot of effort into it. I'm sorry, I just don't see any connection, at least anything we can follow up on."

I didn't tell them about the piece of blue ribbon, and I felt guilty for withholding it. I'd given Sebastian's jacket back to him before he left. Even if I did tell them, it would be his word against mine. And what difference would it make? If it was really Bedelia's, it indicated that she was already there, at the beach, when we were… but there was no way to know if she was alive or dead. It's like that math problem about the cat in the box, where the cat's state is completely unknown and therefore, the cat is both living and dead, in equal parts, until observed. The truth is the police probably already knew the time of death; but if it was *after* we were at the beach, that would mean we *could have* saved her somehow. Maybe we were meant to save her. But at that point my brain grew tired with the endless possibilities.

I felt like the blue ribbon was meaningful to me, it symbolized something, but I couldn't quite wrap my head around what, and I didn't want to sound stupid trying to explain it. Besides, Sebastian had been with us all day; he didn't have time to kill a girl and lay her body out like that. It wouldn't do any good to make Jackie and Derry suspicious of him. Or at the very least, I should talk to him first.

Where was he, anyway? Was he avoiding me? Or had he disappeared as suddenly as he'd arrived? Maybe he left with no word. Maybe I'd never see him again. I put my palms on the table and forced myself to take deep breaths to calm down.

"Don't look now, but the popular table keeps looking over here," Jackie said, nudging me with her elbow.

"The popular table?" I asked.

"All the cute, sportsy guys. Mostly the hurling team and their fanclub," Derry nodded, pointing with his chin.

I looked over at the table—they were typical teenage boys. Cute maybe, but nothing like Sebastian. Roisin and Brianna were sitting with them, along with a few other girls I didn't recognize. Roisin's eyes were puffy, like she'd been crying, and I could hear her talking about how Bedelia used to be one of her best friends, and how sorry she was that they'd drifted apart. Part of me suspected she was faking it for attention and sympathy, then I felt like a bitch for thinking that.

The guys at the table were mostly ignoring her and casting undisguised looks of admiration in my direction. Two of them started shoving each other and nodding towards me. One of them took his hat off and ran his fingers through his wavy blond hair, then came over towards us.

Jackie whispered, "That's Brody. Hurling team captain."

"Hurling—?" I sent her a look, but Brody was already standing in front of us. His blue eyes fixed on me, and he smiled with boyish confidence.

"Hi," he said. "Clara, right? I'm Brody. We haven't been introduced, but it's a small school so everybody knows who you are. I'm glad you're making friends..." he nodded towards Jackie and the others.

"So listen, the guys and I want to invite you to our hurling match after school. It's a home match, on campus. The field is behind the school, Jackie and Derry know where."

"Hurling... that's like, lacrosse, right?"

"Not exactly," Brody laughed. "But kind of."

I glanced behind him to find Brianna and her friends glaring at me. Hanging out with Brody wasn't going to win me any favors.

"There's usually a party after, at least if we win. You're welcome to come. I know the timing is weird, after what happened to Bedelia... but, well, we can't cancel the game."

"We'll be there," a deep voice said behind me.

I turned to see Sebastian as he sat down next to me. He was wearing slacks and a crisp white button-down, with sleeves rolled up to the elbows. As always, he looked like he'd stepped out of a fashion catalogue.

Brody looked confused, his confidence wavering.

"Uh, yeah. Great," he said. He gave me another look and a smile. "Well, talk to you later then."

I smiled at Brody, hoping Sebastian was paying attention. Why did he have to appear just when another guy was showing interest in me. Was he being possessive? *I thought he didn't like me like that.* And did he even notice my sudden change in appearance? I couldn't tell, since he had hardly looked in my direction since sitting down.

I ignored him and turned to Jackie.

"Are Brody and Brianna... together?" I asked.

"I don't think so, though maybe casually, if you know what I mean. Looks like Brianna has other plans for him. Watch out for her, she can be a bitch."

"Can be?" I asked. "I thought it was her default personality."

Sebastian said something I couldn't hear to Patricia and Derry, and they burst out laughing.

Does he hit on everyone? I was pissed off at him, but not sure why. My mood was tanking by the second. I was about to stand up and leave, when I felt Sebastian's hand on my thigh, keeping me seated. Then he leaned in and whispered.

"We need to talk."

Crap. He was going to have 'the talk,' and say he just wanted to be friends, or explain why he couldn't be with me. That he had a girlfriend or something. I didn't want to hear that.

"There's nothing to talk about," I said, trying to scoot away from him. He kept the pressure against my thigh. The warmth from his hand spread up my leg, lighting my whole body on fire.

"You know I found that ribbon on the beach, right?"

I'd already convinced myself that Sebastian had nothing to do with Bedelia's death, and now, looking into his eyes, I believed him. But there was something else he wasn't telling me, something he was holding back. And that's not what I wanted to talk about. I wanted to talk about us. Did he like me, or not? What the hell had he meant when he said he was *forbidden* to be with me? But it seemed trivial to be more worried about his feelings for me, than whether he'd just murdered someone.

I didn't trust myself to say anything, so I clenched my jaw and brushed his hand off my leg. Just then I felt eyes on me and turned to see Ethan, sitting by himself against a window, watching the interaction. He let our eyes meet for a second, then scowled and practically ran outside, slamming the doors behind him. I glanced around the lunchroom. Ethan wasn't the only one staring. I saw at least a dozen pairs of eyes on Sebastian and me. I needed some space.

I got up from the table and crossed the cafeteria. As I walked past a group of girls, I heard Roisin say loudly, "Who gets a makeover on a day like this? I mean, did you see those contact lenses? It's like, 'Look at me!' – and while the rest of us here are in mourning. What a slapper."

I glanced in their direction and saw that they were all looking at me. Roisin gave me a sly grin. *What did I ever do to her?* I ducked my head and hurried past them. I did not have the bandwidth to deal with them right now.

In the afternoon I had Modern Languages for the first time. Yesterday should have been the first but I'd cut school. The teacher, Miss Olivia Lynch, had noticed. When I walked through the door, she started speaking to me in French. Then she switched to what sounded like German, and then some incomprehensible gibberish. I stood there with a blank look on my face.

"You can't speak French, German or Gaelic? Since we didn't see you in class yesterday, I'd naturally assumed you were already fluent in several languages. Pity. I guess it's true what they say about American education." My cheeks flushed red as the other students giggled at my expense.

She let me stand there for a few moments, pretending to shuffle papers on her desk, before looking up at me with an exasperated expression.

"I need a seat," I prompted. I was relieved to see Patricia was in this class with me, and I was eyeing an empty seat next to her, but I didn't know if I could just sit where I liked or if Miss Lynch had a seating chart.

"Well there are several to choose from," she said with a wicked twinkle in her eye. "Just don't sit in one that's already occupied. In Ireland, we like to get to know someone before jumping in their laps."

12

"I cannot believe she said that to you." Patricia grabbed my hand after class. "The first one was mean, but she's harsh on lots of students. But that second thing...unbelievable."

Jackie was furious when she heard. We'd agreed to meet and walk over to the hurling match together after school. "That was totally inappropriate. She doesn't even know you! She's implying, what, you're a slut just because you're American? She should be fired."

"She's not the only one. Roisin called me a 'slapper' earlier. Same thing right?"

"Yeah, but Roisin is a jealous bitch," Patricia said. "And she likes Brody, who basically just asked you out."

"So I had it coming..." I said.

"It doesn't *excuse* it, but it does *explain* it." Jackie agreed. "But Miss Lynch is a teacher, she should be fired. You should report her."

"I'm giving everyone a pass today," I said. "On account of my new look. But I swear, I didn't do anything special. I woke up this morning and looked like this."

I pointed to my eyes, "No contacts."

I held out my hair, "No hair dye."

"Okay, that's weird," Jackie said. I could tell she didn't quite believe me.

"Even so, think about what you're saying," Patricia said. "It's fine for people to treat you like shit because you're *prettier*? Or assume you're a slut because boys want to have sex with you? That's ridiculous."

She was right, but at the same time, Patricia had had years of experience being hot and dealing with haters. And my situation was different; it happened overnight. Of course people were going to assume I'd done it to myself for some reason.

"Can we just forget about it and enjoy the game," I asked. "Please?" Jackie gave me a hug, and Patricia pulled a flask from her back pocket. She'd changed into a pair of ass-hugging jeans for the game.

"This will help," she said with a smirk, taking a deep swig. "Kyle gave it to me, we need to get our pre-game on." I took the silver container from her; the liquid burned my throat on the way down and I coughed.

"We definitely need to work on that," Jackie said, patting me on the back. "If you're going to fit in here, you've got to be able to drink whiskey with a straight face."

Other students joined us on the way to the field behind the school. Jackie introduced me to Conner, Tristan, Brian, Declan, Megan, Kiara...and more I couldn't remember. The mood had shifted. During the day things had been somber, but now everybody just seemed excited about the match. Sebastian showed up at my side, silently. One minute I was looking for him, the next minute he was in step with me like he'd always been there.

He and Jackie started talking, and it bothered me more than I wanted to admit. He was charming, as always, and teased her without being openly flirty. *Why isn't he talking to me?* I took another swig of whiskey. Patricia and Kyle were making fun of American football, running around the field and tackling each other. He lifted her up off her feet and she pushed him away, then they fell on the grass, laughing. They were so happy together, I felt a stab of bitterness. I'd give anything to be that close with someone. But the whiskey was warming me up, and the mood of the crowd was contagious.

Rows of wooden bleachers stood along the side of the field. After we found our seats, Derry started explaining the rules of the game to me. It looked like a soccer field, with nets at both ends for goals. Sebastian disappeared for a few minutes, and came back with snacks for everyone. He handed me a drink, then, when he thought nobody was looking, I saw him sniff the popcorn. *Why does he do that?*

"Players use a stick, the one that looks like a pizza paddle, called a 'hurley' to pass around the ball, which is called the 'sliotar.' They can either get it into net, past the goalie for a three point goal, or over the net between the tall posts for one point."

"Just tell me which direction we're going so I know when to cheer." I grinned.

"That way," he said, pointing to the left.

I tried following the game when it started, but it was chaos. Players could hit the sliotar with their sticks; balance it on the end of the stick and run with it; pass or hit it with the palm of their hands; even kick it down the field.

"It's so fast! It reminds me of Quidditch," I said to Jackie. She rolled her eyes at me. At least I could tell where the ball was, and we stood up and cheered whenever Ballymoney High School scored.

It was a close match, but just before the timer ran out, a burly player sent a wide pass forward. Brody swung his hurley, swatting the sliotar straight past the goalie. The timer ran out, and we won, 14 to 12. The crowd erupted in cheers, and our group all celebrated together. I even hugged some kids I didn't know. Out on the field, Brody's teammates lifted him up on their shoulders. While he was being carried off field, he pointed his hurley straight at me and smiled.

I stopped clapping, my cheeks flushing red. Jackie nudged my shoulder and I heard Patricia giggle. I looked up at Sebastian, part of me hoping he'd be jealous, but he was chatting with a girl I didn't know. Just then, however, he looked over my shoulder and his eyes widened. I whirled around as a hand shot out and slapped the cup I was drinking, spilling Coke all over the front of my white shirt and neck. I shuddered as the cold, sticky liquid ran down my skin and dripped on the ground.

"Oops. Sorry," said Roisin, standing in front of me with a smug look, one her hand on her hip. Then she took off down the steps, laughing. My skin tingled everywhere the Coke had splashed. Time seemed to slow down, and I was acutely aware of the cold liquid on my neck and chest, as the Coke soaked through my shirt. I felt each drip form; it was like I could sense gravity pulling the liquid down towards the ground. I felt each solitary drop splatter against the dusty cement of the bleachers, and the tiny wet molecules swirling in the air from the impact. Suddenly I could feel all the other drinks around me; their consistency and texture, their heaviness. It was like my awareness had widened somehow. The lights and colors around me seemed much stronger and brighter than before, like the world was suddenly brought into focus.

Roisin was down on the field talking to Brody. Next to her was a large water cooler full of Gatorade. A few players lifted it up, getting ready to pour it over their coach, and I could feel the liquid splashing around in the container, the momentum building as the boys tilted it forward.

My eyes narrowed and I clenched my fists together. My attention seized on the Gatorade and I reached out towards it with my fingertips, thwarting the forward momentum and shifting it, guiding it, *aiming* it. It splashed over Roisin with a resounding slap we heard from the bleachers, drenching her from head to toe.

She stood in shock, her mouth hanging open. Her clothes were now a sticky orange color. The boys were laughing and patting each other on the back. They all thought it was an accident. *It must have been an accident.*

"Come with me," Sebastian grabbed my wrist and whispered harshly. "NOW."

His voice was so firm and serious, I didn't question it—I was still in a daze by what had just happened. He dragged me over to the snack booth and pushed me behind it so we were hidden.

"Stay here," he commanded.

A minute later he was back with a stack of napkins.

He blotted them against my neck, shoulders, and chest. He paused, and I saw him smirk, which suddenly restored my modesty.

I grabbed the napkins and pushed him back.

"Make sure you get it all. You can't let any moisture stay on your skin."

"Did you see that?" I asked.

"Yeah, pretty funny."

I bit the inside of my lip.

Did he mean, it was funny that Roisin got hit with the Gatorade, or funny that I'd done it?

But how could I have done it? People can't do things like that. I finished drying myself off and tossed the napkins into the trash.

"What are you doing here anyway? I thought you made it clear you weren't interested in me. Though you and that girl you were talking to seem to have hit it off."

"I have zero interest in her or any other girl, anywhere on earth," he said. "As for you...I didn't say I wasn't interested."

"Oh yeah, it's *forbidden*, right? What does that even mean? I've kind of had it with your cryptic bullshit," I said, glaring at him.

"I just meant, my family, wouldn't approve" he said lamely.

"What, they don't like Americans?" I crossed my arms.

"They don't like humans." He ran a hand through his hair.

Wait... what?

There was a long pause, as I tried to think of a witty rebuttal, but I had no idea what he was talking about. "Whatever," I said, shoving past him. He blocked my path with his arm and pushed me back.

"Listen," he said, grabbing my wrists. He pinned me up against the fence. "You need to be careful. You have no idea what you are, or what you're capable of. It's not safe." His face was inches from mine, his green eyes burning with determination. I'd never seen him look this serious. His grip was hurting my wrists, and I realized for the first time just how powerful he was. Why was he getting angry at me? I hadn't done anything to him. *Not safe...* was he trying to protect me? Or was he afraid I'd hurt someone else?

"Why do you care?" I hissed back at him. "You don't even know me."

"I know what you are," he said.

What I am?

"Then tell me! Who are you—what are you doing here?"

He chewed his lip, which made him look infuriatingly sexy. His skin smelled like he'd just been swimming in the ocean; briny and a little spicy. Like seaweed and shrimp cocktail, with a slice of lemon. His body pressed up against mine; one of his knees between my legs, hitching up my already short skirt. My body ached to bend into him, to push my hands under his uniform and run my palms over his bare chest.

Instead I blurted, "You're hurting me. Is this what you did to Bedelia?"

I don't know what made me say it. I was just angry, and tired of everyone keeping secrets from me. I expected him to yell back at me, or tell me I was being stupid. Instead he released my wrists and sank back like I'd named his worst fear. I was totally unprepared for the look of guilt in his eyes, and for the first time, I was terrified of Sebastian. He may not have killed Bedelia himself, but I was pretty sure he knew who did. And he thought I might be next.

"Just...try not to get into any trouble. Okay?" He backed away. "And don't trust anyone." Then he stormed off and left me there, my back pressed into the fence, breathless with desire and haunted by unanswered questions.

13

I couldn't stop thinking about what happened with Roisin and the water cooler. Nobody seems to have connected it with me at all—maybe it was an unlucky coincidence. A fluke. But Sebastian's reaction had to mean something. Why was he so concerned about getting the Coke off my skin? What had he meant by all his dire warnings? I could no longer pretend it was meaningless; something was going on, and Sebastian knew more than he was telling. What it was, I had no idea. But I needed answers, fast.

I felt like I was unravelling. My sudden change of appearance indicated that whatever happened to my mother was happening to me too. And if I wasn't careful, soon *I* might be on the run, leaving a trail of dead bodies behind me. But how could I protect myself if I had no idea where the danger was coming from? Was Sebastian really involved in Bedelia's death somehow? Was he a threat to me and my friends? Or was *I* the threat?

For the next several days, I tried to recreate the connection I'd felt with the Gatorade. I left the tap water running and watched it swirl down the drain. I could still feel the water, like I could then, but not as much. I pointed to it and curled my finger. *Come.* I waved my hand and beckoned. Nothing. The stream of water ignored me.

Nothing happened when I showered, either. Apart from my perfect complexion, darker hair and mesmerizing eyes, I felt pretty much the same as before. *Is this what my mother went through?* Liam said things got strange before she left, and she turned into a woman really quickly. But other than my looks, there didn't seem to be anything remarkable about me.

Or so I thought. A few days later, eating breakfast with Aedan, I noticed something else. I could feel his mood so much clearer—the ancient melancholy of a broken heart, the mild anxiety of work projects, his love for me but also the overprotected worry, fear almost, that something bad was going to happen.

I thought it was just him, or just me, but it stuck with me at school. When talking with people, I could feel their moods. I wasn't psychic: I couldn't read their thoughts, just broad emotions. I could almost taste them in my mouth. Salty, sweet or bitter depending on the mood. It was kind of like what I felt when I was singing—an awareness of people's reactions to my voice. But now I felt it all the time.

I wasn't sure who I could talk to without sounding crazy. Even confessing to Jackie and Derry seemed risky; I'd only known them for a few weeks. And what was I going to say, "I think I'm starting to read minds? And have telekinetic powers?" They would think I was in shock from the death of my parents and had created a fantasy world.

I hadn't told Sebastian anything about my mother or grandmother, nor the note or the photograph. So why did he think I was in danger? From what? If Sebastian wasn't going to give me any answers, I'd just need to find some on my own.

I spent hours trying to find Barbara Dubbs online, but she was a dead-end. I even asked at the post office for a forwarding address. They told me she'd moved abroad years ago. I didn't have any leads to follow.

I couldn't get Sebastian off my mind. I was drawn to him in a way I'd never felt before, and it was eating me up inside. When I bumped into him at school, his eyes felt full of meaning, like he had so much to say. But he kept his lips firmly sealed and his jaw clenched, like he was trying not to talk to me. It was agonizing.

I tried to distract myself with schoolwork. Geography, with Mrs. Davinia Geraghty, actually was pretty interesting. She wore glasses and had blonde hair, but looked like a little mouse—petite and quick to startle. We were learning the history of the United Kingdom, and the different races and civilizations that had ruled Ireland, and how they'd divided up the territory.

I also began studying languages in earnest. Olivia Lynch still treated me with disdain, and sometimes outright hostility, but I made sure to keep up with the lessons and turn in homework on time. I couldn't pronounce half the words in French correctly, and German grammar made my brain hurt. But for some reason Gaelic came more naturally to me.

And I always had choir to look forward to. Mrs. Tierney doted on me, and it was the only place I really felt like myself. I'd been avoiding my new friends: there was so much I couldn't tell them, and casual conversations weren't even remotely interesting. I couldn't handle being social and pretending that everything was normal.

I started eating lunch in the library, doing homework or reading, but nothing could take my mind off Sebastian or the strange changes I was experiencing lately.

Trying to make some sense out of everything, I took out a notebook and made a list of what I knew so far. I tried to diagnose myself as if I had a disease, by listing the symptoms.

What's wrong with me?
1. *I look different since I turned 16. Beautiful. Darker hair...*
2. *I feel more. I sense things, people's moods and emotions...*
3. *I may have magical powers over Gatorade...*
4. *Sebastian may not be human...*

I almost crossed that last one out, but I couldn't forget what he'd said after the hurling match: that his family wouldn't like me because I was *human*. What did that make them?

When Derry told us about the Fomori, he'd called them legendary creatures. *That didn't sound human to me.* It was a starting point, anyway, and something to occupy my time. I looked up the Fomori on Google and pulled up the Wikipedia page. Like Derry had said, Fomori meant 'of the sea.' They were a race of mythological people that came before the first gods, like the Titans.

Next I used the library computer to find a big book of Irish mythology. It was shelved in the oldest section of the library, where all the books had leather bindings. The book I was looking for had an embossed pattern on the front cover, that had nearly been worn flat. The inside was filled with delicate ornamentation. I flipped it to the section on the Fomori and began reading.

Partholon and his followers were the first to invade Ireland after the flood, but the Fomorians were already there. Then came Nemed and his followers, who also encountered the Fomorians when they arrived. Nemed defeated them in several battles, killing their kings Gann and Sengann, but two new Fomorian leaders arose, living in Conand's Tower on Tory Island.

So the Fomorians were here first, and then other races came and tried to drive them out. I googled Tory Island. It was off the northwest tip of Ireland, about sixty miles away from Portballintrae. The pictures displayed a rugged landmass with steep pillars of rocks jutting out from the sea.

After Nemed's death, the Fomorians enslaved his people and demanded a heavy tribute: two thirds of their children, grain and cattle. Nemed's son gathered an army of sixty thousand, rose up against them and destroyed Conand's Tower, but the Fomorians attacked them with a huge fleet, and there was great slaughter on both sides. Then the sea rose over them and drowned most of the survivors: only thirty of Nemed's people escaped in a single ship, scattering to other parts of the world.

I was skimming over the text, but one line jumped out at me:

The sea rose over them and drowned most of the survivors.

Seas don't usually act so serendipitously. It was mythology of course, but I couldn't help thinking about what happened with the Gatorade. The Fomori came from the sea, and were driven back into the sea when the human clans began to arrive and press for land. It could mean they were a sea-faring tribe, and just got into their boats and sailed somewhere else. But if they were from the sea, maybe they could actually *influence* it. Enough to rise up and swallow their enemies? A lot of people still believe Moses did something like that. And then there's the biblical flood; and the disappearance of Atlantis for that matter.

Atlantis, seriously? I checked myself. I was in dangerous territory if Atlantis was my next lead. I was reading too much into the text. Then again, the only reason I was reading this at all was to try to find answers to the things I'd been experiencing recently—things that a few weeks ago I never would have believed were possible.

After Nemed's people fought with the Fomorians and were washed away by the sea, the next group mentioned were the Tuatha Dé Danann. Their first king was the half-Fomorian Bres, the son of Ériu of the Tuatha Dé Danann and the Fomorian prince Elatha, who had come to her one night by sea on a silver boat. But Bres turned out to be a bad king, who forced the Tuatha Dé to work as slaves and pay tribute to the Fomorians. Another leader, Nuada, was made king after his arm was replaced with a working one of silver, but the Tuatha Dé's oppression by the Fomorians continued.

Bres asked his father, Elatha for help restoring his kingship, but he refused. So Bres turned to Balor, a more warlike Fomorian chief living on Tory Island, and raised an army. The Tuatha Dé Danann also prepared for war, under another half-Fomorian leader, Lug. His father was Cian of the Tuatha Dé, and his mother was Balor's daughter Ethniu. Balor, who had been given a prophecy that he would be killed by his own grandson, locked Ethniu in a glass tower to keep her away from men. But when he stole Cian's magical cow, Cian got his revenge by gaining entry to the tower, with the help of a druidess called Biróg, and seducing her. She gave birth to triplets, which Balor ordered drowned. Two of the babies either died or turned into the first seals, but Biróg saved Lug and hid him away. As an adult Lug gained entry to Nuada's court through his mastery of every art, and was given command over the army.

The next battle was fought between the Fomorians under Balor and the Tuatha Dé under Lug. Balor killed Nuada with his terrible, poisonous eye that killed all it looked upon. Lug faced his grandfather, but as Balor was opening his eye Lug shot a sling-stone that drove his eye out the back of his head, wreaking havoc on the Fomorian army behind. After Balor's death the Fomorians were defeated and driven into the sea.

My eyes were starting to glaze over. It was difficult to keep all the history straight, if you could even call it history. But it seemed like the Fomorians *were* another race, and that they *did* have magical powers of some kind. It also seemed true that there were marriages between the races that led to half-blooded heroes: humans with special powers or abilities. The Tuatha Dé were related to or closely allied with the Fomorians... until the Fomorians used the Tuatha Dé as slaves, and demanded tribute from them. So Lug rose up against the Fomorian armies led by his grandfather Balor, killed him like David killed Goliath, and freed the Tuatha Dé. If it was the same tribute that had been collected earlier, *two thirds of their children, grain and cattle*, no wonder they revolted.

"Fomorians, huh?" I'd been so enthralled with the book, I hadn't noticed Ethan approach until he was standing next to me, reading over my shoulder. I coiled away from him reflexively. He raised his eyebrows, and his long dark hair fell to the sides of his face.

"Didn't you warn me to stay away from you?"

"I may have been a little harsh." He smiled, but there was tension behind his eyes.

"You think?" I said.

"Listen, I'm sorry, alright? I was sure you were going to tell the whole school about... the other day."

"I didn't tell anyone. They wouldn't have believed me anyway."

He nodded. I realized he'd basically just confirmed that he was doing something unusual, instead of denying it like he had before. I thought about what I'd watched him do with the leaf. He definitely had some of the answers I needed, but he'd been such a jerk, I hadn't thought he'd tell me anything. Maybe if I could earn his trust, he'd let something slip that would help me understand what was happening to me, and how to control it.

"I'm doing research for a school project," I said, turning the book towards him, "but it's hard to keep the history straight. The

Fomorians were like another race that lived in Ireland before. Do you know anything about them?" I pressed, arching an eyebrow and curling my lips into a grin.

"More than most," he said, his shoulders relaxing. He grabbed a chair and spun it around, sitting on it backwards. "My mother is kind of obsessed with the history of Ireland, I grew up hearing all the stories and legends."

"Are they just stories?" I asked. "I can't tell. All the stories sound mythological, full of supernatural elements. But legends are usually based on something. I mean there were wars, between the Fomorians and the…." I looked back down at the book, "the Tuatha Dé. That part sounds like history. There were probably two groups of people fighting over the land, right?"

"Until the Fomorian leader and his poisonous eye were defeated by the half-blood Lug." He grinned and I realized he was teasing me.

"Right," I said.

We were close enough that I could smell his scent. It was like pine needles, sandalwood and fresh dirt after a rainstorm.

"Don't tell me you've never heard of the Tuatha dé Danann, children of the Goddess Danu," he said.

I looked at him blankly.

"Most people call them the Elven, or Fae."

Fairies? No freaking way.

"I didn't see anything like that in the stories," I said.

"Probably because it's internet rubbish." He said. "The Tuatha Dé were powerful warriors, who could do things most people can't even imagine. But that was a long time ago. These days, they've been reduced to tiny, invisible winged beings that can only be seen by sensitive idiots in their gardens."

That seemed a little harsh, but I didn't want to contradict him.

"But... why were the Tuatha Dé fighting the Fomorians? They seemed to be allies at first. Bres and Lug were both the result of unions between both races, but they fought against each other."

I felt like I was missing something. It couldn't just be about land.

"Let's just say that the Tuatha Dé and the Fomorians were dependent on each other, and resented it. Did you read about the Training of Cúchulainn yet?"

"No, what's that?"

"A medieval text, it's more famous than this stuff. Cúchulainn is an Irish hero, kind of like Hercules. He was the son of Lug, so he still had some Fomorian blood. He finishes his training and goes to look at the sea. While there he sees a great assembly gathered on the beach, and among them, a beautiful woman—the most beautiful he'd ever seen—but all the people around her were crying. He asks her what's going on, and she tells him that every seven years, the Fomorians demand a tribute: the first-born of the king's children. And it's her turn to be sacrificed."

"Soon they saw a great ship appear over the waters, and the damsel's people all fled from her, and not a single person remained except Cúchulainn. On the ship was a warrior—dark like the devil—and he was laughing."

"'Why is he laughing like that?' asked Cúchulainn. 'Because,' said the damsel, 'he thinks it's excellent that you've added yourself to the tribute this year.' Cúchulainn gets angry, and says, basically, 'come here and say that to my face.'"

"So the big man comes ashore and reaches out for Cúchulainn, but Cúchulainn raises his sword and strikes off the man's head, his first kill after finishing his training."

"That reminds me of the story of Perseus and Andromeda," I said, when Ethan had finished.

"And that's the problem with mythology," Ethan said, nodding, "Most of the cool stories that people could dream up were shared, traded, stolen, and added to make their tales more interesting. So you usually have to dig behind anything too incredible to believe, and look for the historical root."

"There's a historical root to that story?" I asked.

"Sure," Ethan said. "The Fomorians still ruled a lot of humans, and demanded sacrifices, even after they were driven out of Ireland. Cúchulainn stopped it. That's why he's a hero. But he probably couldn't have done it if he was just a normal human. He did it because, like his father, he had Fomorian blood."

There was a heavy pause, and Ethan gave me a pointed look, as if he was trying to communicate something. Whatever it was, I didn't get it. None of this made any sense. And I couldn't see how these fantastical stories had anything to do with me.

"I'm Ethan, by the way." He held out a hand, introducing himself as if we were strangers. I realized we'd never been formally introduced, so I shook his hand.

"Clara," I said, trying not to smile at our mock civility. I was surprised by how comfortable I was with him. His punk rock act and bad attitude had put me off at first, but after listening to him recount Irish legends, it was hard to see him as anything other than a book geek.

But my stomach churned with suspicion. Why was he being so nice to me all of a sudden, when he'd always been such a jerk before? Was it the way I looked now? Was he hitting on me? Or was this something else?

"When is your report due?" he asked.

"Huh?" I said.

"Your paper, for school—?"

"Oh, um, it's a long term project. A couple weeks I guess."

"You should come over to our house, talk to my mom. She knows everything, and has a whole shelf full of old books you can't find anywhere else."

He's inviting me home to meet his mother?

That didn't mesh with the bad boy biker I'd pinned him for. Maybe all the chain and leather was just a screen to keep people out. Sebastian had warned me to be careful who I trusted, but right now Ethan seemed like the safer bet.

"Thanks for the offer... I'll think about it, in case I don't find what I'm looking for."

If only I knew what I was looking for.

***

After third period I stopped in the washroom. I spent more time studying myself than was strictly necessary, but I just couldn't get over my new appearance.

"Looking for your horns?" a voice said behind me. *Roisin.* "Don't worry, I'm sure they'll show up soon." There were dark circles under her eyes. She came closer and stuck a finger in my face. "I know it was you," she whispered. "At the match. I don't know how you did it. But I know." She looked manic. Unsettled. I felt her paranoia wrap around us like an inky cloud.

I swatted her hand away. "You spilled that Coke on me, on purpose, and now you're accusing me of—what, having magical powers? Even if I could have done something like that, don't you think messing with me might be kind of stupid?" I tossed my backpack over my shoulder and stormed out of the bathroom, leaving her behind me with her mouth open.

During the last period I was momentarily surprised to find a priest at the head of the classroom, but then I remembered *Religious Education* was part of the curriculum here. I wondered if I should have prepared something, and quickly brought up the school's website on my phone for a description of the class. Apparently its aims were to help 'young people develop a positive sense of themselves and their beliefs, along with a respect for the beliefs and values of others, while presenting students with chances to develop their personal understanding and enhance their spiritual and ethical awareness.'

That didn't sound too bad. Then I noticed the name of the teacher and my blood ran cold. Father *Murphy*. I looked up at the man in front of the classroom. He was young, in his early forties probably. I sighed a breath of relief. He couldn't be the same Father Murphy that had disappeared along with my grandmother, he was way too young for that. He was wearing a long black cassock and the traditional white collar. I realized suddenly I should probably know what that meant. What was he, Catholic? Protestant? I didn't know much about the religion of Northern Ireland, except that people took it very seriously. I'd have to be careful not to say the wrong thing.

"Last week I asked what you thought the *most ethical* religion was, and why," Father Murphy said when class began. His hair was almost bright red, and clashed comically with his serious outfit. "Let me be clear, the answer isn't to decide that one religion is *more ethical* than any other; it's just an interesting departure point to keep in mind as we look at the history of religious movements and the leaders that started them. I want you to leave aside, for a moment, any personal beliefs you have about one religion being *right* or *true*, and I want to look at each religious system in terms of Bentham's Utilitarianism. In other words, which is the most *practical*? Which has the most measurable *benefits* to the widest number of people? What does each religion say about morality and right action, and do the actions of believers of that religion follow the code of conduct? Is there space for disobedience? What happens when someone acts wrongly? Punishment? Forgiveness? Are there exceptions to the rules?"

This is not was I was expecting, but Father Murphy's enthusiasm held me captive. He walked around the classroom with his hands behind his back, and his eyes shone with excitement.

"For example, most religions have a code of conduct that applies to *equals*, but is often withheld to large groups of people, especially those of other cultures or races, on the grounds that they are outsiders, and so aren't protected by the rules of the religion. It's tempting to think that things have changed since the crusades, when thousands of Christians flocked to the Holy Lands, raping and pillaging their way through Muslim territories. But here in Ireland, we have very recent, very violent examples of how conflict can be justified and exacerbated by religious belief. So again, I ask… does belief *cause* racial and cultural violence? Or does it simply *fail to prevent it?*"

We spent the next hour in small groups, talking about the ethics of religion—or at least other people did. I kept my mouth shut. My parents had never really been into religion, and I hadn't thought much about it. I didn't feel inclined to start now.

A girl in my group raised her hand. "I think your question is kind of misleading," she said to Father Murphy. "All humans sin, we can't help it, but it doesn't matter who sins the most or what causes them to sin. All that matters is which religion offers *redemption*. We owe a debt for our lives, a debt that could only be paid with blood—and that's what Jesus did for us."

I stifled a groan. I did not need to hear about Jesus right now. I had bigger fish to fry.

"But the system of blood sacrifice and atonement started long before Jesus," Father Murphy said. "Under Hebrew law, almost everything is purified with blood, and without the shedding of blood there is no forgiveness of sins. Traditionally, the whole idea was that humanity had been taken hostage by Satan in the garden, and the devil needed to be paid ransom. But that fell out of favor, and in the 11th century, a monk named Anselm displaced the devil entirely and made the payment of Jesus' blood about a debt to God's honor. But the passages in the Bible describe the payment given to a captor, to release a captive."

Blood sacrifice. Atonement. Redemption. I couldn't help thinking about Bedelia. Derry had called the murder ritualistic. I didn't believe any of this stuff, but a lot of other people did. Was Bedelia sacrificed for something? Killed to pay some kind of debt?

After class, one line kept repeating in my head like a chorus. *Without the shedding of blood, there can be no forgiveness of sins.*

14

All this mythology was too big for my brain to think about, and was probably a waste of time. Seriously, what did my family, or me, have to do with ancient warring races of Ireland? It suddenly seemed more important than ever to find out what really happened to my mother. I kept coming back to the facts.

Colin was possibly my mother's boyfriend, who had been killed the night she disappeared. My grandmother Phyllis had also disappeared under mysterious circumstances. And now there was me. The threatening messages, the mysterious incidences that defied logic. It gave me goosebumps every time I thought about it. Was there some kind of family curse I should know about? If the Tuatha Dé took over Ireland by defeating the Fomorians, and they had some kind of supernatural powers because of their Fomorian blood, is it *possible* that there were still descendants, to this day? If so, is it *possible* that my grandmother and mother had been caught up in some kind of... supernatural race war?

It sounded ridiculous. But on the other hand, history seemed to be repeating itself. One girl was already dead, and I didn't want to be the next. I'd been carrying the photograph with me everywhere, but was mostly too scared to ask anybody. That had to change. Of course I should have just asked Aedan, but every time we were alone together, I could feel his persistent melancholy. Even if that note my mother left him hadn't been the whole truth, I didn't want to make things worse for him. I could go back and talk to Liam again, but wasn't sure what that would accomplish.

At school, I practiced reading people's emotions, and I was getting pretty good at it. I could sift through a crowd, matching moods and feelings with particular speakers. It excited me when they said one thing but felt another. I never knew how much people lied.

After History class one day, I decided to put it to use. I waited around and showed my mother's picture to Mr. Halpern.

"I saw on the faculty website that you went to school here," I said, "I think you must have been classmates with my mother."

He took the photograph from me and adjusted his glasses. "My oh my," he sighed. "This takes me back."

"Do you recognize the kids in the photo?"

"Sure, that's Liam. I still see him every few weeks at the pub in Portballintrae. That's Colin Blake, Barbara Dubbs and... *Oh.*" He looked me over with fresh eyes. "This is your mother? Branna Daly? I didn't make the connection until just now, but you look so much like her."

I could feel traces of his adolescent longing as he thought about my mother. *Was everybody in love with her?* "Do you know where Barbara is now? Or Colin's family?"

"Barbara moved away for college I think, and never came back, as far as I know. Overseas, last I heard. The Blakes live a short drive from here, towards the coast. I don't know much about Colin's family, I was never close to your mother or any of these kids. You might say we ran in different circles."

"Do you know how Colin died?"

Mr. Halpern looked around apprehensively, then sat down at his desk. "I heard the rumors, of course, but I'm not sure it's proper for me to be repeating them all these years later."

"Please, I'm just trying to understand why my mother left Ireland. Was there some connection between her and Colin? Were they dating?"

"Well, like I said, I wasn't exactly on friendly terms. But yeah, I suppose they were. Or everybody thought they were. That last year, they hung out all the time. They skipped classes, got whatever they wanted. We thought they were cool. Teen rebels, you know. But, most of the other kids were also afraid of them, and I suspect the faculty was too."

"Afraid of them? Why?"

"Nothing, just rumors, you know how kids talk. Special powers and nonsense like that. There were some things that went on, that seemed unexplainable. Whenever something happened that seemed to defy logic, somebody would say 'Where are Colin and Branna?' It was kind of a running joke."

"And the day Colin died?"

"There was always something suspicious about that case, actually, but the family hushed it up. They didn't want an investigation. Family matter, they said. He was buried on private land. Awful stuff, his own mother found the body. The next day

Branna was gone as well. Her father swore she'd left earlier, so she couldn't have had anything to do with it, but of course the police tried to track her down for questioning. But since the family didn't want to force the issue, and Branna was gone anyway, everybody just kind of moved on."

My fingers were twitching. I wanted to be taking notes. This wasn't exactly new information, but it did put things in a new light.

"Thanks," I smiled. "That was really helpful."

"Ask Father Murphy," he said. "He'd know more about the funeral arrangements, and what happened to the body and what not. You should ask Olivia, too."

"Miss Lynch?" I asked, startled.

"She was around then too. Same year as your mother and I."

Of course she was.

I asked my other teachers and some of the school staff about the photograph, but nobody else had been around long enough to remember my mother. Except for Miss Lynch. As I sat in her class, trying to keep up reciting and conjugating French verbs, I could feel the hatred radiating off of her. And it wasn't the sharp, metallic feeling of new anger, this felt more like a tin can, buried underground and containing radioactive material. I should have picked up on it before. *She knew my mother.* But I couldn't bring myself to ask her. I did everything I could just to avoid being humiliated again.

At lunch I told Derry and Jackie what I'd learned from Mr. Halpern. We hashed out the things we already knew, but it seemed like we were just going in circles.

"I still think we should just go to the police," Jackie said for the hundredth time.

"But there's no evidence that Bedelia is connected to Clara in any way," Derry countered. "It was probably just a freak event. Someone passing through."

"What about Colin's family?" Jackie asked. "Mr. Halpern thinks they might still be around. Maybe they could give you answers."

"I thought about that," I said. "Though that's not a conversation I want to have. 'Hi there, can you tell me how your son died, and whether my mother had anything to do with it?'"

"Besides," Derry said, "if for some reason there was something going on, and Clara does have some kind of weird family feud going on, it's probably best to let sleeping dogs lie, right? Don't go poking the hornet's nest? Most people here know you as Clara Clark, right? So unless you tell them, they won't even know you're a Daly."

I wanted to believe Derry was right, but I felt deep down like things were just getting started.

"At least we know why Miss Lynch hates you so much," Jackie said. "Something must have happened between her and your mother."

"Whatever it was, I don't think she'd tell me about it," I said.

"Then we have to find out what was going on between them. We can ask Liam again, or—"

She cut off when she noticed me peering over her shoulder. I was watching an old man trimming the hedges; the one in the photograph I took on the first day of school. I'd caught him staring again.

"Hey Jackie, who is that?"

"Galen. School caretaker."

"How long has he worked here?"

"Ages, as long as anyone can remember."

Maybe he wasn't ogling me, I thought suddenly. *Maybe he knew my mother.* People said she stood out. Maybe he remembered her. When I got up and started walking towards him, he turned his back and got back to work.

"Galen?"

He turned around, and took off his hat, sheepishly.

"Yes, miss?"

"My name is Clara, I'm a new student here."

He nodded but didn't say anything.

I took out the photo and handed it to him.

"My mother used to go to school here. Branna Daly. This is her with some of her friends."

"Mighty shame..." he said looking at the ground. "Tried to stop them."

My ears perked up. "What? Do you know something about my mother? Do you know why she ran away?"

"Don't know nothing, miss. Just the gardener."

He pushed the photo back to me, looking around furtively, then turned back to the bushes. I was sure he knew something.

"What about the Fomori?" I said, changing tactics. "Can you tell me anything about them?"

He blanched and looked around him desperately, bringing the shears up in front of him defensively. I took a step back.

When he saw there was no immediate danger, he breathed deeply and looked me in the eyes again. "Myth. Folklore. Old stories is all."

"I'm researching them… for school. Can you tell me any of the stories you know? I would really appreciate it." I could feel his emotions. Horror, fear. He was *afraid* of the Fomorians, which meant he believed they were real. And dangerous.

I took a risk and put my palm on his arm, as I would to calm a skittish horse. I tried to communicate feelings of peace and well-being, and I could feel his mood calm considerably. Apparently I could do more than just feel emotions.

"The old folks say, you can catch one by stealing her cap. Hiding it like, so she can't go back. Make good wives. Until they don't. Those stories always end in tragedy. Swore I wouldn't tell. Can't talk more, gotta work," he stumbled, nervously, turning his back to me again. I returned to the table.

"Well?" Jackie asked.

"He knows something. But he's spooked."

"He didn't tell you anything?"

I shook my head no, but I felt like Galen *had* told me something. I just needed to figure out what.

15

Aedan had written a note excusing me from the pool. Unfortunately I still had to suffer through regular gym class, but on pool days I had drama instead. The teacher was William Cahir—a melodramatic, posturing moron. He'd started the first class by reciting Edgar Allen Poe, holding a fake skull prop, then flapping around the theater yelling "Caw, caw, caw!" and making us do the same. It was ridiculous, but also fun to loosen up and be silly. And I liked the improv games.

I came out of the theater smiling and squinting at the brightness. I almost ran into the silhouette blocking my path.

"Coffee?" Sebastian said, holding out a cup of Starbucks.

I took the warm cup, but didn't say anything. Was this an apology? We hadn't spoken since the hurling match.

"Let's take a walk," he said, holding one hand out to me.

I hesitated.

"You have something better to do?" he asked, with a sly smile.

I'd been trying to forget about Sebastian, but all my feelings for him came rushing back instantly. Was he trying to be friends now? Or maybe he was finally ready to give me some answers? Hoping this was the case, I took his hand and let him pull me up. My heart started pounding as I realized we were holding hands. I pulled my hand away from his grip and wrapped my fingers tightly around the coffee cup.

He didn't say anything at first, we just walked together, sipping our coffee and enjoying the weather, which was overcast but clear.

"Your mother is the one who was Irish, right?" he asked finally. I nodded. "What do you know about her?" he asked.

"Apparently, not a lot," I said. "But I've been trying to find out more. It hasn't been going well," I sighed. "She grew up here, just her and Aedan, until she was sixteen. Then there was an accident of some kind, involving a boy she was friends with, maybe her boyfriend. He died, and she ran off to America."

His eyes widened, and I expected to feel shock or curiosity from him. I felt nothing. I realized suddenly that I couldn't read his moods like I could with other people. The emotional silence heightened the awareness of my own feelings.

"And your grandmother?" he asked.

"Phyllis," I said. "I'm not sure where she came from, I didn't know anything about her until recently. She was beautiful, and she liked to sing. She disappeared when my mother was four... and the town priest disappeared at the same time."

His face remained impassive.

"Come on," I prompted. "Both my mom and grandmother involved in potentially lurid scandals? What do you think the chances are for me?"

I was half joking, but he didn't smile when he glanced over at me. Instead, his eyes were apprehensive, like he was thinking *that's exactly what I'm afraid of.*

"And the ocean?" he asked.

"What about it?" I said.

"You've never... lived near it before?"

I scoffed. "Not likely. My mother always seemed to be keeping me away from it." Then I told him about the day at the Oregon coast, the day I'd almost drowned. Other than Beth, I'd never told anyone about it before.

"But now that I'm living so close to it," I said, "I feel a calling towards the ocean—like it's inviting me to come in. I know it sounds crazy. I've developed an uncanny sense of direction. No matter where I am, I can feel it, beating against the shore like a heartbeat. Relentless. Constant. I could spin around with my eyes closed and still know exactly how far away the coast was, and in which direction."

He nodded, sighing, and ran his fingers through his perfect hair. As he did I got a scent of sunshine and lemons. I imagined his long, slender fingers running through my own hair, grabbing me tightly. I resisted the urge to reach out and touch him, and instead crossed my arms in front of me.

"How about your parents?" I asked, trying to turn the conversation away from me. I realized I still knew practically nothing about him. *Except that he's the hottest guy in the world.*

"My mother is kind, sweet, gentle. Beautiful. I remember her singing when I was little, and playing games. Hide and seek. My father…"

His face darkened, and I could see his neck muscles straining.

Daddy issues, I noted.

"My father is in the military. He wants me to be tough. Hard. He used to yell at my mother for being too soft with me. He wanted me to train all the time."

"Train for what?" I asked.

"Now that I'm older, he wants me to be a soldier, like him."

"And you don't want to," I guessed.

"Be a soldier? Follow orders and kill someone I don't know because somebody else told me to? No thanks."

I nodded, Sebastian didn't seem like a warrior type. He was strong, there was no question, but I couldn't see him hurting people.

We'd circled the school and were now passing the hurling field. The team was practicing, and a handful of students were sitting on the bleachers, soaking up one of the last sunny days of the year. A few girls followed Sebastian and I with their eyes, and I could feel their envy reaching out after us. I'll admit, it felt good. I wasn't used to having other girls be envious of anything I did, apart from singing.

Suddenly there was a loud crack and a whizzing noise. I ducked instinctively, but Sebastian hardly flinched; he just reached up and snapped the sliotar out of the air casually.

"Sorry about that, sport," a voice called from the field. *Brody.* I could sense his emotions. Malice and mirth, with a dangerous splash of testosterone and male bravado.

"You need to be more careful," Sebastian said, his voice low, like gravel. It carried across the field. "You could have hit her."

Brody closed the distance between us, and said quietly, "I wasn't aiming for her."

He stood there, leaning the large wooden paddle over his shoulder, as if daring Sebastian to start something. Two of Brody's friends, Mark and Ryan, came to stand beside him, ready to back him up. Sebastian tossed the ball a few feet in the air and caught it again.

"So how's this sport work, anyway? You take this ball, and you put it through that goal over there, right?"

Sebastian's arm shot out and the ball went flying past Brody's ear, shooting straight and fast across the field. Brody dodged, then looked behind him just in time to see the ball sink under the opposite goalpost.

Brody's jaw dropped.

"That's over 130 meters..." Mark said, his eyes wide.

"Is that good?" Sebastian asked, dryly.

"Just under the world record for throwing a ball, distance-wise," Ryan said, also impressed.

Brody scowled, and pointed with his hurley. "You're a freak. It was a trick of some kind. We'll finish this later." Then he turned and walked back on the field.

Just then I remembered the story I'd been reading in the library, about Lug and the sling-stone that destroyed Balor's poisonous eye.

"Ok," I said, "Let's cut to the chase. What are you?"

"What do you mean?" Sebastian said, his eyes shifting. The warm glow I felt earlier vanished. I thought we'd shared a moment; I thought he was opening up to me. But he still wouldn't tell me the truth, whatever it was. And I couldn't bear to hear any more lies. I decided to lay all my cards on the table.

"You freaked out at the game when I spilled that Coke, and I'm pretty sure you know I caused Roisin's Gatorade shower somehow. And just now, you threw that ball further than any normal human had any right to. Meanwhile I've become a human mood-meter, which means I get to always know exactly what people feel about me all the time. Which, basically sucks, since most guys are just thinking about what they'd like to do to me in this uniform. Oh yeah, and I've been receiving threatening notes."

"What notes?" he asked sharply.

I pulled the two notes out I'd received from my school binder, and Sebastian scanned them quickly.

"This one is probably just high school meanness. A girl I'm guessing, who feels threatened by you. Where did this one come from?" He asked, holding the other note up, the one that looked like calligraphy on a scrap of parchment.

"It was pinned to my front door," I said.

"This one is probably a spell, though incantations are usually longer, so it's hard to say without seeing the rest of it."

For a minute I thought he was joking. I looked at him like he was from another planet.

"A spell? Like – witches and magic wands and Gandalf?"

"Who's Gandalf?"

"Forget it," I snapped.

"I don't know very much about human magic, but it means that somebody here probably knows what you really are, and that means you're already in more danger than I thought," he said.

"There you go again with the *human* stuff. Do you seriously not think you're human? Or is this some weird role-playing game you're into? And why do you keep saying *what I really am*? What am I?" I was getting worked up. I bit my lip, trying to calm down, but his refusal to let me in was infuriating. He reached up to stroke my cheek but I slapped his hand away.

"Don't you dare," I said, raising my voice. "I fell for that once before, but I'm not going to be one of those girls who faints in your presence. When you decide you want to tell me the truth, I'll be waiting."

I turned my back and walked away from him, seething.

I'd opened up to him, but he still didn't trust me. He was either keeping secrets, or insane. Maybe both. I was frustrated of being kept in the dark, by people who obviously knew what was going on.

I decided to stop waiting for answers. Sebastian said he didn't know about human magic... but I had a feeling I knew someone who might.

16

"This came for you," Aedan said, gesturing at the envelope on the table when I got home. It was addressed, and stamped. My heart quickened when I saw the name on the return address: Mrs. Dubbs, Portrush. I tore the envelope open and took out a thin piece of stationery paper.

Dear Clara, my name is Barbara Dubbs, I was a close friend of your mother's. I have something for you, please come see me. Discretion is advised, so come alone. I hope we can meet on Pier 11 in the Portrush harbor, there's a coffee shop near there. Does Saturday Oct. 10th at 4pm work for you?

My heart pounded in my chest. So she was still around—and in Portrush, that wasn't far at all. How did she know about me? Did my mom keep in touch with her?

When I left school I'd had the semblance of a plan: confront Ethan and ask him about the note that Sebastian had called 'human magic.' But this was *way* better. I was sure Barbara would have answers for me.

Jackie texted me in the evening.

Saw you at school with Sebastian. Must have gossip. Coffee?

We planned to meet at a coffee shop in downtown Bushmills called French Rooms. Derry would come too.

Need a ride?

I checked Google maps and saw it was only about a mile away. I was still buzzing with energy from the note.

Nah, I'll bike it. Fresh air will do me good

They were waiting for me when I arrived. Derry had on a gray jacket and a scarf. With his golden hair, he looked debonair and European, much better dressed than your average teenager. And I envied Jackie's long, forest green jacket, which looked expensive and contrasted perfectly with her bright red hair. I felt underdressed—and I was sweaty from riding over. But I didn't care about my looks.

The coffee house was cute, with polished dark wood, red leather padded seats and brick walls. It was filled with art nouveau posters, old clocks and knick-knacks. Next to a book shelf was an old teddy bear on top of three antique suitcases. It smelled like lavender and fresh bread, and even had a fire place. We slid into one of the round compartment booths, which gave us privacy. It was like being in our own little room. I got a latte and a blackberry scone, and Jackie had black tea with lemon. Derry was eighteen already so he got a hard cider.

It was nice to be together again, just the three of us. Hanging out with Derry and Jackie felt effortless, unlike the stress I felt sometimes at school. I could finally relax and be myself. But once we started talking, I realized things were different now: I had secrets. A lot of secrets. I didn't tell them about what had happened with Roisin, or my weird confrontation with Sebastian afterwards. And I didn't tell them what I'd seen Ethan do with the leaf, or our private chat in the library. I wanted to, but I didn't really have anything concrete to say; plus, without any evidence, I would probably sound crazy, especially if I let them know I could feel their emotions on my tongue like snowflakes. In fact, I realized, they were both *worried* about me. This was an intervention. They thought I was just being sad about my parents, or maybe about boy troubles, and they were trying to take me out and cheer me up.

I did my best to smile and keep my mood positive. Soon I was telling them about Mr. Cahir's antics in the drama department, and we had a good laugh about it. Derry seemed uncharacteristically energetic, I guessed he had a secret of his own.

"Derry, you seem... really happy tonight," I said. "Almost glowing. Did something happen?"

"Derry has news," Jackie said. She nodded at him, prompting him to share.

"Well, it's just that… I met this guy," he said, eyeing me for a reaction. *Jackie was right.* I gave him a warm smile, and he looked relieved and continued.

"We met at a club, last weekend, and hit it off. Went out for a date last night. And…I really like him."

"That's great," I said, smiling, though I had to force it a little bit. *At least somebody is finding romance.* "What's he like?"

"Older, in his twenties at least. Handsome. Well dressed. He says he's a banker but he never seems to be working." I nodded, letting Derry share. But I couldn't stop thinking about the note I'd gotten from Barbara Dubbs. I'd finally be getting answers. And she said she had something for me, maybe something my mom left for me? The note had told me to come alone, but it seemed foolish not to tell anyone where I was going. I was about to pull it out and show it to them when I heard Roisin's voice. I leaned out of the booth, but froze when I saw who she was with. *Sebastian!*

I ducked back into the booth, trying to ignore the pain in my chest and my trouble breathing. What was he doing here… with *her*? I gripped the edges of the table tightly. The room started spinning.

Jackie peeked out of the booth and saw them too.

"Oh, honey…" She reached across the table and squeezed my hand. "Maybe they're just friends."

"Should we ask them to sit with us, or would that be… really awkward?" Derry asked.

I shrugged. I was too stunned to speak.

"Let's just pretend we didn't see them," Jackie said.

I tried to shrug it off, but I couldn't concentrate on the conversation anymore. I kept poking my head out of the booth to spy on them, and strained my neck eavesdropping.

Why should I even care who Sebastian goes out with? It's not like we were together. *But Roisin?*

After a few minutes I looked up and saw Roisin lean in close to him, her perfect curls brushing against his flawless skin, whispering into his ear.

I felt like smashing the table in half. Although I had no right to feel it, I couldn't control my rage. At that moment, all the salt shakers in the café, on every table, started wobbling and spinning, filling the room up with a warbling hum. I was practically shaking. *Was I doing this?*

"I'm sorry, I need to get home," I panted, sliding out of the booth quickly. "I'll see you at school tomorrow."

I charged straight past Sebastian and Roisin and rushed out of the coffee shop, slamming the doors behind me. I'd just gotten on my bike and flipped up the kickstand, when Sebastian grabbed the handlebars, blocking my path.

"Roisin asked me to meet her here," he said. "There's nothing going on between us."

"I know what I saw," I said. "She's enamored with you."

"I can't control that, humans are attracted to our kind."

"Poor you. It must be hard, having girls throw themselves at you all the time," I said, narrowing my eyes.

"I can't help the way they react to me… just as you can't help the way they react to you. Face it, you're different now. Anyway, we were talking about you."

Roisin and Sebastian were talking about me?

I scoffed and rolled my eyes.

"She warned me to be careful around you, because you're different. She told me you were a witch. That you had magical powers. I was trying to talk her out of that idea, when your little display inside interrupted us."

"Get out of my way." I tried to push the bicycle forward, but it didn't budge. Sebastian's grip was like a vise.

He leaned closer, inches from my face. "You have to learn to control your emotions," he whispered softly. "Public outbursts like this are going to get you killed." *Was he threatening me?*

I shoved him out of the way, much harder than I'd expected. As he stumbled backwards, I jumped on the bike and pedaled away furiously.

17

On Saturday I convinced Aedan to let me take a bus by myself to Portrush. He offered to drive but I said I needed to learn the bus system. I could have biked it—it was only about four miles—but I didn't want to ride home alone after dark. I told him Jackie and Patricia were going with me. Girl's day. Shopping trip. I hated lying, but Barbara told me to come alone, and I needed time to clear my head before meeting her.

I thought I'd be able to handle Sebastian's rejection gracefully, but instead I'd had two public altercations with him. The second, a jealous outburst which—thanks to Roisin—was sure to be on everyone's lips at school on Monday. How did I become *that* girl? I was always so good at keeping my feelings bottled up.

I was certain Sebastian was keeping secrets from me—and that made him a dangerous mystery. Why did he keep talking about humans like he wasn't one? And what did he know about Bedelia that he wasn't sharing? Did it have anything to do with why my mother left Ireland, or how Colin died, or what really happened with my grandmother?

And then there was that thing with the Gatorade, and the salt shakers in the café. Both happened when I was upset. Sebastian said I needed to control my emotions. But why? I'd tried moving all sorts of objects with my mind, but I could never do it on purpose. What was the connection?

Getting upset about high school drama felt self-centered when there were so many other things that should bother me more. I was sick of how clueless I was about everything. I hoped Barbara would have some answers.

I got into Portrush early to do some research; there was an antique bookstore in town I'd looked up online. Maybe I could discover something new before my meeting. The smell of musty old books and leather greeted me when I pushed the door open. Stacks of books were piled high against the walls, and in the back of the store were glass cases with leather bound manuscripts. The wooden floorboards bounced under my feet as I approached the desk.

"Do you have anything on the Fomorians?" I asked the clerk. "I'm looking for something that talks about where they came from."

He peered up at me over his glasses. At first I thought he was going to refuse to help me, but then he took a good look at me and he gave me a dopey smile. With my new beauty, I realized, I was going to get what I wanted most of the time. I wasn't sure how I felt about that. He walked to the glass cabinets in the back and unlocked them. I had a feeling he wasn't supposed to.

"This one was written in 1882, so be careful with it," he said.

I almost dropped the book when I saw the title.

Atlantis, the Antediluvian World, by Ignatius Donnelly

"Wait—this is about Atlantis. That can't be right."

"Check out chapter seven." He grinned, gesturing to a study area with benches and tables.

I sat down and flipped open the heavy tome, leafing through the pages until I found the right section.

> CHAPTER VII
>
> THE IRISH COLONIES FROM ATLANTIS
>
> *In the Irish historic tales called "Catha; or Battles," as given by the learned O'Curry, a record is preserved of a real battle which was fought between the Tuatha-de-Dananns and the Fir Bolgs, from which it appears that these two races spoke the same language, and that they were intimately connected with the Fomorians. These particulars would show the race-identity of the Fir-Bolg and Tuatha-de-Dananns; and also their intimate connection, if not identity with, the Fomorians.*

I skimmed the rest of the chapter. According to Donnelly, the Fomorians were early Atlanteans—whatever that meant. When Atlantis sank, some of them had escaped in ships, and landed in Ireland, where they offered sacrifices to Poseidon, the founder of their civilization.

And they liked silver, which they seemed to be able to use in miraculous ways. Sailing in silver ships? A king with a silver hand, capable of moving fingers? I was so absorbed in the book I didn't realize the light was dimming. It was almost 4pm. I put the book back and practically ran for the pier. I got there just in time. There were a few people walking around, eating ice cream or popcorn. Some fishermen sat on the end of the pier casting out lines. *Why meet way out here?* I wished I knew what Barbara looked like.

As I waited, I tried to organize all the questions I wanted to ask. Whether my mom had gone through these changes as well, and how she handled them. About Phyllis and where she came from. What really happened with Colin. Ten minutes passed, then another ten. The pier was thinning out, but still I waited. As my mind wandered, my awareness slowly reached out under the water, almost subconsciously. I'd felt a connection with the ocean since my birthday, but now that I was right above it, I could sense things deep below the surface. I suddenly realized I could feel a host of underwater creatures. To my left there was a small school of sleek silver fish, about five inches long. A handful of shrimp and a grumpy old lobster scurried across the sandy bottom. I could feel the currents and waves of the ocean and how they interacted with the flora. It was incredible. I reached my hand out over the water.

I called out with my mind, instinctively. Almost immediately the school of fish started jumping, one at a time at first, then two or three together, then more and more. Soon it was like a silver rainbow of flying fish, and I was their conductor. I laughed out loud. I was so amazed at was happening, I didn't notice I wasn't alone until I saw the flash of the knife.

Time seemed to slow down, and for an instant I saw the weapon clearly—the dark, gleaming blade engraved with an intricate pattern that curled down its length. I watched it slash my arm, cutting a deep gash. Before I could feel the pain, someone shoved me from behind and I stumbled off the edge of the pier. I fell forward into the water, flailing my arms and legs. The fish I had controlled a moment before swam in a frenzied circle around me, as my blood flowed like thick red ink in the water.

I tried to kick back up to the surface, but my clothes, heavy with water, pulled me down into the darkness. I was going to drown. Already my lungs were bursting from trying to hold my breath, and I was seeing stars.

Wait, not stars. My befuddled brain protested. There was a colorful sparkle, all around me, but especially on my cut arm. I was sparkling, shining in a prism of colors, like a Christmas tree. And then—just before everything went dark—I thought I saw Sebastian, down here with me in the murky depths.

18

I woke up gasping for air and clutching my throat. The last thing I remembered was being in the water, the colorful lights against the darkness. And then... *Sebastian.* But how much of it was real?

I was in my bed, at Aedan's house, wearing boxers and a Hello Kitty tank top. My hair was dry. *How did I get here?* I remembered the bite of the knife as it cut into my arm; the blood oozing from the wound just before I was pushed into the water. But both my arms were perfectly smooth. I couldn't find the slightest mark. Had I dreamed it all?

I got up and put on a burgundy skirt with gray tights, and a dark green knit sweater. The landscape out my window was foggy and wet. I could barely see to the ocean. I put my fingertips to the window and watched my breath fog up the glass.

"Morning, sleepy head," Aedan said as I left my bedroom.

"Hey, what time is it?"

"Almost eleven."

It was Sunday morning.

"Oh. Um, do you know what time I came home yesterday?"

"Around 8pm I think. You must have come in without me noticing; I was getting worried about you but I checked your room to get Patricia's phone number and you were already in bed sleeping. How was Portrush?" He handed me a cup of coffee.

So I *had* gone to Portrush yesterday, to meet Barbara Dubbs. Which meant, everything else had probably happened as I remembered it. I shivered, recalling the flash of the knife, and sinking into the water—my worst nightmare come true. I pictured my body, laid out on the pier, framed in a ring of flowers. I shook my head to clear my thoughts. Someone tried to kill me. *Why wasn't I dead right now?* At the very least, I should be bruised and traumatized. Instead I felt... *pretty good.*

I realized Aedan was still waiting for an answer.

"Um, good. Fun," I said.

"Do you have plans for the day? Homework?"

Sebastian's face flashed through my mind again. He was swimming towards me through the darkness, the strange colored sparkles lighting up his face. But that couldn't have really happened, could it? I wasn't going to be able to think about anything else—least of all homework—until I got some answers.

"I think I'll go visit a friend," I said. "You?"

"Gotta finish a house," Aedan grumbled. "Without disturbing Mrs. Miller's flower bushes."

I nodded, even though I didn't know or care who Mrs. Miller was. Before I left, I grabbed the strand of pearls from my desk and wrapped them around my wrist. I wasn't sure why, but they made me feel safe. Protected.

I took the bike through town in the direction Derry had driven us. The fog grew thicker outside of town, until I could barely see a few yards in front of me. I found the turnoff, but I couldn't see the Runkerry house until I got close to it. Then it loomed out of the fog like the bow of a great ship. There was a raven sitting on the black iron fence. At first I thought it was a statue I hadn't noticed before, but when I wheeled up it opened its black wings slowly, stared at me for a minute, then took off. I watched it flap away until it disappeared into the fog. I thought of Mr. Cahir's performance in drama, but somehow it didn't seem funny anymore.

Then I realized I didn't have Sebastian's phone number. Jackie had added him as a friend on Facebook, but for some reason I hadn't. There were no buttons on the front gate, and it was locked. I stood there for a few minutes, feeling stupid. I considered shouting his name, or climbing over the fence, but both seemed extreme. And what exactly was I going to say, anyway? I was just turning my bike around when I heard a voice behind me.

"Leaving already?"

Sebastian was leaning against the gate, looking overdressed as always in a navy blue jacket, a tan vest, checkered shirt and dark jeans. I'm sure he wasn't there a moment ago. The last time I saw him, he told me I was going to get myself killed. My brain screamed at me that he could be responsible, but somehow in my heart I knew it wasn't true.

"We need to talk," I said.

"Want to come inside?" he said, unlocking the gate and swinging it open.

I pictured us sitting on the couch awkwardly.

"Can we take a walk?" I suggested.

He shrugged and gestured towards a path that led along the coast. As we neared the water, the wind grew stronger. My hair blew across my face and I pulled it to the side, wishing I'd brought the red ribbon to tie it up.

Sebastian pulled up his collar. His figure cut a stark silhouette against the rugged terrain of the Irish coast, and the swirls of mist around us. We both seemed to be waiting for the other to speak first.

"What happened yesterday?" I asked finally.

"How much do you remember?" he replied.

"Somebody tried to kill me... and you, I think you saved me." I didn't offer the other possibility—that he'd been the one to push me in.

As we approached the water, the roar of the ocean made us raise our voices. I thought he was going to deny it, but finally he nodded.

"You are far too interesting to let die."

"You saved my life because you think I'm interesting?"

"Well, more like *mildly irritating*," he said. "Maybe *vexing* is a better word for it."

"How did you even know where I was?"

"I saw you leave your house— " Sebastian said, looking guilty.

"You were *following* me?" He nodded. I didn't know whether to feel flattered or disgusted.

I decided to push on. "I was in the water, and I saw lights. Sparkling, colorful lights," I continued. "And I know you're going to blow it off or say it was oxygen deprivation, but I didn't imagine the hands that pushed me in the water, or the knife that cut me. That was real. If I'm in danger, I deserve to know why, and I think you have the answers."

Sebastian's eyes were greener than I'd ever seen them when he turned to look at me. "You don't know what you're asking—"

"I'm asking for the *truth*."

"Sometimes, ignorance is a happier choice."

"Facts do not cease to exist because they are ignored." I threw back at him—a quote I'd memorized years ago.

Sebastian sighed and ran his fingers through his hair. "If I tell you, you'll never be able to go back to the person you were before. You'll change."

"Look at me." I pointed to my eyes and tugged my hair. "I'm already changed."

He didn't answer, and I could tell he was wrestling with himself.

"Listen, I'm scared and I don't know what's happening to me. But it seems like you do. So if you want to protect me, if you want me to be careful, then tell me the truth."

"You'll hate me when you know," he said softly, peering out over the ocean. "You might hate yourself."

I grabbed his arm and pulled him closer, so I could look into his eyes.

"What am I?" I demanded.

The wind and water pounding through the nearby rocks sounded like a human scream.

He furled his eyebrows, and I thought for a second he was going to yell at me. But then he slumped his shoulders.

"The old term is *merrow*. Sometimes called Fomori, or sea people. Popularly known as mermaids."

I clenched my jaw to keep it from dropping open, and my fingers twitched as I typed out the word *m-e-r-m-a-i-d-s*. Coming from Sebastian's mouth, it sounded so ridiculous I almost laughed out loud. Only the look on Sebastian's face stopped me. "There's no such thing as mermaids," I snapped.

Was he making stuff up just to throw me off track? The thought of him lying to me made me furious, and my blood started pounding in my ears. I couldn't explain what I'd done to Roisin, or how my arm had healed so quickly. But *come on*. I scanned his face for even a hint of humor, but it was as solemn as a grave.

"Wait, you're saying... are *you* a mermaid?"

I pictured Sebastian with a fish tail, and the result was comical. My lips twisted up in a grin.

"Merrow is the gender neutral term," he corrected. "Like human."

I decided to humor him. "Even if I was ready to believe that mermaids were real, which I totally am not, how can I be a mermaid—a merrow? I can't even swim."

"Well, you aren't really. Merrow are born in the sea, and have two merrow parents. You're a mennow, a mixed breed, with some human and some merrow blood."

"Shouldn't that be *women*now?" My attempt at a PC joke was feeble at best. Sebastian ignored me.

"As for not swimming, I'll admit that threw me at first; most of your kind are drawn to the sea and love the water. But it seems your mother tried to keep you or anyone else from finding out what you really are. Besides, we don't mature for sixteen years, so you may have always seemed perfectly normal—until recently."

This couldn't be happening. I was willing, momentarily, to accept at the very least that Sebastian believed himself to be a... merrow. Everything about him seemed flawless and magical. *But me?* There was no way I was anything other than exceptionally ordinary.

I thought about my childhood, searching my memories for any indication of abnormality. "My dad's parents were definitely human," I said. "They died when I was young. I remember visiting their house. My grandpa kept a jar of peanut butter cookies. My grandma collected little porcelain dog statues."

"And your mom's mother?" Sebastian said, with a knowing look. I remembered the pictures I'd seen of my grandmother. Those big dark eyes, the shiny black hair, the silky smooth skin. My mother had looked like that too. And now, so did I—except for the color of my eyes, which were Artic blue.

Could this really be the explanation—that my grandmother was a mermaid? I wasn't quite ready to believe it. "At school, you said you hadn't seen my kind in decades. Are there others like me?"

"It's not uncommon, or at least it didn't used to be. Merrow and humans have been interacting for thousands of years, and often produce offspring."

"How is that even... biologically possible?" I asked.

"Want me to show you?" He raised one eyebrow with a smirk.

I'm talking to a mermaid, and the first question I ask is how they have sex? I changed the subject, my cheeks turning red.

"Before I was pushed into the water, the attacker cut me." I rolled up my sleeves to show him my bare arm. "It's totally healed. There's no trace. That's impossible."

"Not for us," he said.

I was feeling unsteady on my feet, and looked around for a place to sit down. But I had one more question.

"But... even if all this is true, why would anyone want to kill me?" I had just arrived in Ireland. I couldn't fathom why anyone would do me harm.

"Merrow blood is powerful, almost magical above water. There are still humans who remember the old ways, and they'll stop at nothing to get it."

"They tried to kill me... for my blood?"

"Actually, I don't think they were trying to kill you," he said.

I snorted, "Sure, it was just a love slash," I said. "Those happen all the time."

"The knife, and then pushing you into the water...I think they just wanted to know for sure. They saw the lights, or saw you survive. And now they're certain what you are, which means, they'll come again. And next time won't be a test."

"Wait, but if they're after me for my merrow blood, then you're in danger too, right?" I asked.

"I can take care of myself," he said, with a smirk.

"But why risk it? Why don't you leave?"

I knew the answer before he said it, as he reached up and brushed his fingertips against my cheek.

"You. I'm here for you."

19

There was a picnic table about a quarter mile away from the Runkerry House, on a bluff overlooking the ocean. Sebastian took off his jacket and put it over the wet wood so I could sit down. We were completely alone, and shrouded in fog. I felt like I was in a dream world, where nothing else existed but the two of us.

I was glad that Sebastian was finally talking to me, but how could any of it be true? At first I thought he was just trying to impress me. But he'd avoided telling me any of this for weeks; I was the one pushing for answers. And what about all the things I'd seen recently? Things I still couldn't explain. If he was crazy, so was I.

"You're taking all this rather well," he said, leaning his elbows against the table. The fog was clearing a little. I could see the Runkerry house behind us, and the rock cliffs up ahead, plunging into the foamy green water. A cluster of thin pine trees was on the other side of us, erupting out of a carpet of bright green moss.

"I'm probably just in shock," I said.

Mermaids are real. My mind was still rejecting the phrase. I needed to see some proof.

"Okay," I said. "I have questions."

I got up and sat on the opposite side of the picnic table, leaning forward on my elbows, interrogation style. He smiled and crossed his arms.

"You're a mermaid—a merrow," I said.

"Yes... both my parents were born in the sea."

I gazed down at his legs.

"But you look so... *human.* Do you have a tail? Like, half human, half fish?"

"More like a crustacean actually," he grinned. "Picture eating a piece of shrimp. The outside is tough. Hard. But it slides right off, leaving the soft flesh underneath. It's an exoskeleton—we call them exos—that must be moulted. It's shed during growth, and remade in a process known as ecdysis. Ecdysis comes from Ancient Greek: 'to take off, strip off.' It probably originated with men who watched merrow come to shore, strip their exoskeleton and turn into men. It's possible that the first men to walk on land were really merrow."

"Wait, you mean Darwin got it wrong?" I tried to imagine what an evolution chart would look like with giant crustaceans instead of apes. Sebastian shrugged and continued.

"We have several exos when we're young. We shed one, and go through a growth spurt until a new one hardens. Once we reach adulthood, we can remove it ourselves at will using a process called apolysis; the separation of the old exoskeleton from the underlying epidermal cells. We can do it consciously, with mental preparation. Then it comes off quite easily, like removing a boot. If we don't do it, it has to be ripped off and is very painful, like cutting off our skin. If we come onto land and keep dry, we can pass as humans. But we're weak, vulnerable."

"You don't seem weak to me," I said, running my eyes over his chest and biceps. I felt like I was in science class. I wondered whether Sebastian had ever given a talk like this before.

"But in the ocean, with our exos on, we're nearly invincible. Hardly anything can puncture our exos. Even our fists are protected by a thick layer of cartilage. Our shoulders are powerful because we use them to punch through coral reefs, crack open oyster shells, or fight off larger predators." He held up his fists to show me, and took a couple mock swipes.

"Ever heard of the Mantis shrimp?" he said.

I shook my head.

"Its punch is as strong as a gunshot: so powerful and fast it *boils* the water around it. And their skin is so resilient, the military has been studying their cell structure to make advanced body armor."

"So what you're saying, basically, is that you're a giant shrimp?" I couldn't help teasing.

"A very charming, handsome shrimp," he replied. I blushed thinking about my next question. It was embarrassing, but I wasn't going to settle for half measures. Now that I was in on the secret, I wanted to know *everything*.

"How do you... mate?" I finally blurted out,

His grin widened. He was enjoying himself.

"We come on land and remove our exoskeletons. Under our shells our organs are... nearly identical to humans. If we want children, the females will stay in caves near shore until the eggs are ready, then go into the ocean and give birth. After a few months, they'll grow their first exo, but then they'll need a new one every year for about twenty years. After that, they will stay virtually unchanged for decades."

"Where are your gills? How do you breathe?" I asked.

"They healed over, but will open again once I grow back my exoskeleton. Our lungs function both ways; on land, we breathe through our noses and mouths. Underwater, that windpipe closes and we breathe through our gills, through a separate chamber."

"Show me," I said. I was tired of the biology lesson. I wanted to see it for myself.

He lifted his shirt, and I saw a series of thin horizontal lines that looked like healed scars on both sides of his abdomen. Then he leaned down and picked up a small pebble. He set it on top of the wooden table.

"Ready for the fun stuff?" he asked, with a twinkle in his eyes.

I nodded.

"Keep your eye on this. Don't blink."

For a second, nothing happened. Then a flutter of wind pushed my hair back and the rock vanished. I hadn't seen Sebastian move a muscle.

A second later, it was back; then it disappeared again. Sebastian's grin grew wider as he held the rock up for me to inspect.

"We can move fifty times faster than you can blink. Not all of us, just our arms and hands. Underwater, we need that strength to overcome the water pressure and resistance. But up here, we move so fast it looks like magic. It's mostly good for cheap parlor tricks, but it often comes in useful."

"It's like stopping time," I breathed.

"Sort of. I couldn't catch a bullet. But I could shove someone out of the way. Or reach over and take the gun. I can break through this wood—" He smashed his fist down on the end of the table and broke off a section of the rotting plank. "But if I tried to punch a metal door, I'd break my hand. Still, I'm dangerous. If I got angry or in a fight, I could put my fist through someone's skull. I actually have to restrain myself from moving too quickly, so I don't accidentally hurt someone."

"That's how you threw the ball so far," I guessed.

He nodded, then held up his hand. I gasped when I saw it. It was bloody, with chips of wood sticking out of it. "You see? Weak." He walked over to the edge of the turf and jumped down to the water's edge. He leaned down between the rocks and put his fist in the water. I could see the rainbow colored lights and sparkles shimmering under the water's surface. Then he shook his fist, and came back to show me his hand. It was flawless.

"Ecdysis also allows damaged tissue and missing limbs to be regenerated. That means we heal quickly, if we can get back to the salt water."

"So when the attacker cut me and pushed me into the water..."

"That's the process you saw happening, the lights—ecdysis will heal any wounds first, before it starts regenerating your tail."

A tail?

"Holy crap, I'm a freak." I said, sinking my head into my hands.

"Mennows don't always transform all the way. It depends which genes you've received. And you'll never be as fast as I am, only native merrow are, who grew up underwater and built body mass to counteract the water pressure."

Something Sebastian said earlier was tugging at my brain. *Virtually unchanged for decades.* It suddenly dawned on me that Sebastian wasn't as young as he looked.

"How old are you?" I asked, pulling away from him and tensing my body for the answer.

"About seventy-eight. Still young, for a merrow," he said.

I tried, unsuccessfully, to keep the shock off my face.

78 years old.

I felt dizzy. This was too much to take in.

He reached out and put his hand over mine, squeezing it gently. I ripped it away.

"Are you... immortal?" I asked.

"No, but we live a long time. On average three hundred years, though some merrow are twice that. If we live on land, we age much faster. We need to spend several hours a day in the salt water or we'll start aging."

"Are there more, like me?"

"Not with as much merrow blood as you have." He frowned. "It's illegal for merrow to mate with humans—it has been for centuries. Of course, some merrow still spend time on land. But if they fall in love or want to start a family, they're risking their lives."

I felt my blood chill. "What happens if they're caught?"

"Mating with a human is considered treason. Punishable by death," Sebastian said.

I felt sick to my stomach.

"What if they kept it a secret? What if nobody knew?" I asked.

"After a merrow sleeps with a human, their scent will be altered for months. If they go back into the ocean, they'll be found, arrested, and executed."

"And if they stay out of the ocean…"

"They'll grow old and die," he said.

"But I'm *not* human," I said.

Oops. I just admitted I was thinking about the two of us having sex. My cheeks burned, and I looked away.

"You're not entirely merrow either," Sebastian said. "But, at this point, I'd be killed as a traitor anyway, since I'm not supposed to talk about any of this stuff."

"Wait, they'd kill you just for telling me this?" I said. One of Sebastian's earlier comments clicked into place. *You don't know what you're asking.* I held my breath as he nodded.

"Talking like this to you, about us… it's an open defiance of the laws." He looked away, but not before I saw the sadness in his eyes.

I stood up and pushed away from the table, trying to hide my shame. Sebastian hadn't wanted to tell me any of this, and I'd pushed him for answers. Now he was a traitor to his own kind, and they would kill him for it.

"But, why would you do that?" I asked, horrified.

"Because you asked me to," he said.

The butterflies I usually experienced around Sebastian felt like they'd turned into worms, eating through my abdomen.

"They would kill you for being here with me," I repeated, "But you're here anyway?"

I thought about my mother and Colin; my grandmother and Father Murphy. It seemed that romances in my family were doomed to tragic endings. He nodded, and reached out for my hand. I didn't pull away this time.

"Wait, is that what happened to Bedelia?"

That look of guilt came back to Sebastian's face, and he let go of my hand.

"No, that's not what happened," he said quietly.

"You know who did it," I said.

"Not exactly. But I know why they did it. A long time ago, that was the way some merrow would mark their territory. They'd claim a piece of land. If they didn't want other merrow getting involved in their business, they would put bodies out to warn others away. It's a barbaric custom. It was outlawed by the royal family a long, long time ago, when the merrow decided to disappear, and prohibited interaction with humans."

"Wait, there's a royal family?"

"There was... for thousands of years. Descendants from Poseidon, the first of our kind. But they disappeared, decades ago. Nobody knows what happened to them."

"Bedelia was killed by a merrow?" The words tasted sour on my tongue.

"A twisted merrow," Sebastian said, clenching his fists. "One that enjoys killing. Decorating his kill like that, exhibiting it almost, to the sea. He was daring anyone to stop him. And he knows that nobody will. Without the royal family, nobody cares enough about the humans to stop him."

"But *you* wouldn't do that?" I asked.

"What, kill humans for sport?" He looked hurt. "No, because I'm not a psychopath. Besides, I'm not really interested in humans. I usually keep to myself. I observed, without getting involved."

"Until me," I said.

"Until you." His confirmation flooded my body with warmth. He reached up and tucked a strand of hair behind my ear. "You, I can't stay away from. When I saw you on the cliff, at first I was just curious. Like I said, there aren't many mennows around anymore. But there's something different about you. What you did to Roisin... I've never heard of a mennow with that much power. It shouldn't have been possible. And that's why you're in danger. Until you can control your powers, you'll be a target. Although it seems like it's too late now. Somebody already knows what you are."

I nodded. As crazy as it sounded, what Sebastian had told me so far seemed like the most plausible explanation for the things I'd experienced lately. *But now what?*

"So let me get this straight," I said, my need for order prevailing. "Somebody is trying to kill me for my merrow blood, and some psychopath merrow is killing human girls to mark his territory. And now you're in danger from both the humans, who would drain you, and your own kind, who would execute you."

It all seemed so hopeless, and yet a tiny part of me was thrilled. Sebastian was putting his life at risk, *for me.*

"The law is a little gray in that area, actually," Sebastian said. "If you were a normal human, they'd kill me for sure. Since you're a mennow, they'd probably stay the execution and just punish me. If you could change all the way, and become a full merrow, then I wouldn't have broken any laws... but like I said, that may never happen."

Finally, a solution that didn't involve either of us dying. I didn't care if I was grasping at straws; if changing fully meant saving Sebastian, it was the only option. Besides, what girl didn't dream of becoming a mermaid?

"How do we start?" I said.

"First things first, you need to learn how to swim."

20

Sebastian insisted on seeing me home. He rode my bike and I balanced on the handlebars. When he dropped me off, he leaned in and kissed my cheek.

"There's one more thing I need to tell you," he said.

"What's that?" I asked.

He inhaled deeply.

"You smell amazing."

"Excuse me?" I said.

"That's one thing we don't have underwater; smell. Up here, I can't get enough of it."

That evening, I couldn't stop smiling. Even though my world was just shattered and someone tried to kill me—and even though both Sebastian and I were in mortal danger—at least I wasn't alone anymore. Sebastian's lips on my cheek made me feel like I was on fire. The frustration I'd felt for weeks was gone. As I sat in front of my typewriter, instead of my normal furious purge of confusing thoughts, I felt a deep calm. One thought filled my being, and for the first time in a long time, I had a clear goal.

I'm part merrow, but I've put Sebastian's life at risk by making him tell me. If I can become full merrow, he'll be safe...

Part of me felt like I was throwing my life away, for a guy I barely knew. But I wasn't just doing it for him. Since my parents died, I'd had absolutely no control over my life. If I really thought about it, maybe I'd given up control long before—that day in Oregon when I almost drowned. Since then, I'd always relied on others to take care of me. Maybe it was time to take my life back into my own hands... even if it meant growing fins.

But how exactly does one *become* a mermaid? Sebastian said it was possible, but not certain. And if it really happened, would I be willing to live with the consequences? I decided to research everything I could on mermaids before committing myself to something irreversible.

I opened my laptop and started with Google, pulling up all the pages I could find, and sorting them into chronological order. The earliest mermaid-like figures were the ancient Syrian goddess Atargatis, who watched over the fertility of her people, and Ea, the Babylonian god of the sea. Both had the lower body of a fish and upper body of a human, and were worshipped almost 7,000 years ago. Ea would later be co-opted by the Greeks as Poseidon and the Romans as Neptune.

In one text, Ambia, the monstrous daughter of Cain, had the tail of a fish and could travel by land or sea. The Roman naturalist Pliny the Elder wrote of the nereids. He called them nymphs, but they were half-human, half-fish. Legatus of Gaul once wrote to Emperor Augustus claiming he found a "considerable number of them dead upon the sea-shore."

I took a break from reading to make some tea. Miscreant followed me into my room, and jumped onto my lap when I sat back down at my desk. It was getting late but I couldn't stop searching. Everything I read seemed to suggest that the merrow were older than civilization, even that civilization and technology *had come from* them, as gifts from the gods—Ea or Atargatis. I was surprised to learn that Christopher Columbus had seen mermaids on his trip to the new world, and even John Smith had seen them before he met Pocahontas.

But then things got strange. Mermaids became mythological, fanciful. Nobody had seen one for centuries, so all we had were recycled stories and myths. In 2012 Animal Planet put out a fake documentary, with actors pretending to be scientists, claiming to show evidence that mermaids were real. Despite being attacked by critics as fraudulent pseudoscience, it had been the most watched program in the channel's history. A month after the program aired, the National Oceanic and Atmospheric Administration posted a statement on its website denouncing the supposed existence of the half-human, half-fish beings, saying "No evidence of aquatic humanoids has ever been found."

Modern experts believe that Columbus, Smith and other mermaid-spotting explorers were really just catching glimpses of human-sized marine mammals like manatees and dugongs, but it strained belief that they could be mistaken for humans, unless all the sailors were super drunk (which they probably were, since they drank nothing but beer and rum all day long).

Stories about the merrow were common on sites of Irish folklore, though most of them just talked about how to "catch" a merrow wife. Apparently merrow have special clothing, or at least the women do, called a *cohuleen druith* or "little magic cap" that helps them navigate ocean currents. In order to come ashore, the merrow abandoned her cap, so any mortal who finds it has power over her. She cannot return to the sea until it is retrieved. Hiding the cloak in the thatches of his house, a fisherman may persuade a merrow woman to marry him. But after some "years in succession" she would inevitably return to the sea, her "natural instincts" irresistibly overcoming any love-bond she had formed with her terrestrial family. To prevent her acting on impulse, her husband kept her *cohuleen druith* "well concealed from his sea-wife."

My blood chilled after reading that passage. Could that have been what happened to my grandmother, if she was indeed a merrow? Had Aedan *forced* her to marry him against her will, and she'd abandoned my mother as a child because she couldn't resist the call of the ocean? I hoped that wasn't true.

At school the next day I was practically beaming. I'd been self-conscious before, because I thought I was weird. Now I knew I was different, but it didn't make me strange. *It made me special.*

It seemed like ages since I'd talked to Derry or Jackie. I was glad I hadn't told them about the note from Barbara Dubbs. They would have wanted to know how it went. What could I tell them, that instead of showing up, someone had stabbed me with a knife and pushed me into the water? Although I wasn't certain, in retrospect I'd decided the note was probably sent by someone else, just to get me alone. And how would I explain my instantaneous healing? I couldn't tell them about the merrow without putting their lives in danger. Sebastian and I couldn't help what we were, but Jackie and Derry were safe, as long as they didn't get involved.

I couldn't hear a word my teachers said in class, I was too excited. After school, Sebastian was going to take me somewhere and teach me how to swim. Although I was worried I wouldn't be able to get past my fear of drowning, what choice did I have? Also, somehow my experience in Portrush made my terror less palpable. It was like I'd already lived through it.

"What do you want to be, Clara?" Jackie asked at lunch.

"Um, what?" I'd been thinking of pearls, shells and green eyes.

"For Halloween. We're discussing costume ideas," she prompted.

"You guys have Halloween here?" I asked.

"Are you kidding? Halloween is an *Irish* holiday," Derry said. "It comes from the old Celtic festival Samhain Eve. Immigrants brought Halloween to America."

"Where it got corrupted." Patricia said, smirking.

"Families usually cook a special dinner with boiled potatoes, cabbage and raw onions. We wrap coins and hide them in the potatoes for kids to find," Jackie said.

"Don't forget the barnbrack cake," Derry said.

"The what?" I asked.

"It's a fruitcake that has a rag, ring and coin hidden inside it," Jackie explained. "The rag represents a doubtful financial future, the ring represents impending romance and happiness, and the coin represents prosperity. If you get one of them, that's your fate."

"Do you carve pumpkins?" I asked.

Jackie rolled her eyes at me, "Pumpkins are from America."

"Original jack-o'-lanterns were carved from turnips or potatoes," Jackie said.

"Carving turnips is for kids," Patricia added. "We'll have a bonfire on the beach. It's a huge party, you should totally come."

"Of course she's coming." Jackie smiled at me. "We wouldn't go without you."

"I'm going to be a fox," Patricia said. "I have these furry ears and boots, and a sexy bodice with a mini skirt. Derry is going to be a giant squirrel."

"So I can say I'm looking for nuts," Derry said.

"I want to be Tinkerbell, I think," Jackie said. "Or Athena. How about you?"

"Maybe you should be a mermaid," said Sebastian, with a sly grin on his face. He squeezed in across from me. He had a habit of appearing out of nowhere.

"I'm sure I'll come up with something," I said, kicking him under the table.

"Even if we're not mermaids, we can pretend... with a little skinny dipping," Patricia said. She held her palms up and arched her hips like she was doing the butterfly stroke.

"I'm in," said Kyle, watching her chest bounce under her uniform.

"You can't go swimming," Jackie said. "Didn't you see the news?" When we didn't respond she pulled out her phone and looked up a video. The headline said "Biggest shark attack in history: 17 people injured, 3 dead."

"When did this happen?" Sebastian asked, the color draining from his face.

"Yesterday," Jackie said. She hit play on the video.

A reporter stood on the beach holding a microphone. Behind him, paramedics carried stretchers across bloody sand to the ambulances. "It's a scene of total chaos behind me, and the largest maritime tragedies the little town of Brighton has ever witnessed. I'm here with Professor O'Donald of the Ocean Science department. Tell me, professor, just what is it that makes this incident so extraordinary?"

"Well, you've got to understand, firstly, that Great Whites—and sharks in general, actually—very rarely attack humans. People get the wrong idea, from watching Jaws and shark attack movies, but the truth is, sharks don't like the taste of humans. We're too bony, too hard to digest. Almost all of the so-called attacks were just test bites. And even this only happens when the water is murky or under other conditions when the sharks' senses are diminished."

"So they bite just to figure out what we are, and then don't eat us?" the reporter asked.

"Of the 147 unprovoked great white shark attacks since 1990, only 29 of them were fatal—and almost all of those were from loss of blood. Sharks don't eat humans."

"Can you explain what happened here in Brighton?"

"I cannot. Most sharks would bite a human and then swim away. To see this amount of injuries, in the *same* place on the *same day*...I'm not even sure if a single shark could have done this."

"Are you saying that this the result of multiple sharks?" the reporter asked.

"We won't know that until we measure the wounds and compare teeth marks, but Great Whites don't hunt in packs, so that's unlikely too. But if it was just one shark, there would be no motivation for it to injure so many people at once. Maybe there was something in the water that confused them. But honestly, we've never seen anything like this before."

The video clip ended with a close up of a man's leg. The deep row of gashes in his leg still oozing blood. "I'm just lucky to be alive," he said.

"That's awful," Patricia said. "But Brighton's pretty far south of here."

"Not far enough," Jackie said. "If it happened there, it could happen here."

Sebastian nodded. "Swimming at night would be a very bad idea."

"Ok, fine," Kyle said, groaning. "We get it. But you're robbing me of potentially the greatest experience of my life."

Patricia laughed and slapped his arm.

Derry rolled his eyes, "You guys are dating, you shouldn't need some elaborate excuse to see each other naked."

"And on that note," Kyle said, "I exit. Gotta run, babe." He kissed Patricia and waved to the rest of us. Class was starting soon so we said our goodbyes. Sebastian and I did an awkward, lingering handshake, like we didn't want to let go of each other.

"What was *that*?" Patricia asked after the guys had left.

"You guys are together now?" Jackie asked, raising her eyebrows.

"Kind of. Maybe. I'm not sure," I said.

"Did you kiss him?" Jackie asked.

I shook my head.

"Sleep with him?" Patricia asked.

"I just said I didn't kiss him!" I said.

"You can do either one without doing the other, *darling*." Patricia said. "I don't know how you roll."

She smiled at me and I shoved her. My cheeks were heating up, and I pretended to be too embarrassed to talk about it. *Were* we together? It seemed like it. But if we hooked up, Sebastian would be hunted down and executed by the fish people. But I was happy just hanging out with Sebastian. I wasn't ready for anything else.

In choir class, I wasn't afraid of standing out anymore. Singing was in my blood, it was my heritage—mermaids were famous for singing. And my voice was one thing I could enjoy and show off, without endangering myself. I relaxed and closed my eyes, allowing myself to revel in the feeling of the music. Roisin and Brianna had given me dirty looks at the beginning of class, like they always did, but by the end of it Roisin actually smiled at me. *Weird.*

I was almost to my next class when I heard Ethan's voice.

"Give it back. *Now.*"

Mark and Ryan had him pinned up against the lockers. Brody stood in front of them looking at a piece of paper. *Bullying is alive and well.* Ethan clenched his fists, and I smelled something burning. He twisted to the side and pulled his arms free, then reached out and shoved Brody with the palm of his hand. It was a light push, barely a touch, but Brody flew back and slid across the floor. The piece of paper drifted to the floor. *What gave Ethan the power to do that?* He was holding something with his other hand. Something powerful. I could feel the energy pulsing from it.

"Why you little shit," Brody said, standing up and preparing to charge. "That's *it*."

"Ethan," I called, stepping in front of Brody like I didn't see him. "I need some more help with my paper, do you have time? Oh hey, Brody," I turned and said casually.

I felt Brody's anger, but also his confusion, spiced with a touch of relief. He was happy I interrupted this fight. I sent soothing emotions, like I'd done with Galen, and I watched his face relax. I was getting better at that.

"Oh, hey Clara, you know Ethan?" Brody said.

"Yeah, we're old friends," I smiled sweetly.

"I didn't know that," Brody said sheepishly, rubbing the back of his head. "Sorry."

"We're just playing around. You know how boys are," Mark said. He picked up the paper and passed it to Ethan, who snatched it quickly. But not before I saw what was on it: a charcoal portrait of a girl who looked *a lot* like me. I felt my blood heating up. *Did Ethan draw that?*

"We don't mean anything by it, you know that right?" Ryan punched Ethan on the shoulder. Ethan held his gaze without flinching, his body tense.

"You didn't have to do that," he said after the boys had left. "I can take care of myself."

"So I noticed." My gaze lingered on Ethan's rippling muscles, still taut from the fight. That's twice I'd seen him do mysterious things that looked like real magic. I had a feeling he could take care of himself.

"Picking on you seems pretty stupid to me," I said.

"A year ago I was a scrawny weirdo." Ethan flashed a bitter grin. "I was an easy target, and I didn't fight back. They'll learn soon enough, I'm not the same kid they used to push around."

I nodded, but was only half listening. I reached into my pocket and pulled out the note with the inked message. If he could tell me more about it, maybe I'd figure out who was after me.

"I have a problem, and I have a feeling – an intuition – that you're the only person who can help me," I said.

"I'm busy," he sneered. "Why don't you go ask your *boyfriend*?" The anger on his face was so strong that I pulled away from him. He opened his backpack to stuff the drawing inside, and I caught a glimpse of something else, tucked between his notebooks and binders. An antique dagger, with a white handle, and decorative grooves running down the blade.

21

I had to warn Sebastian. I didn't think Ethan was my attacker—though I couldn't explain where he'd gotten the knife. Maybe it wasn't the same exact one, or maybe he was somehow involved with the same people who were after me... but I was pretty sure he didn't know what I was. When he mentioned Sebastian, I'd felt hot jealousy radiating from him. Plus, there was that picture he'd drawn. I didn't get the impression that he wanted to kill me. But why would he have a knife like that, or bring it to school with him? Unless it wasn't me he was after...

I didn't see Sebastian for the rest of the day, which worried me, though I knew his attendance left much to be desired. We'd agreed to meet at my place after school for my first swim lesson, so I went home, put my suit on under my clothes, and then waited by the window. When he pulled up in a little black car, I was so happy to see him, I gave him a hug.

"What is *that?*" I asked, pointing at the vehicle. The car looked like a miniature hearse, with round edges and sweeping curves along the body. The seats were bright turquoise.

"1957 Austin a35," he said. "A classic."

He held the door open for me and I squeezed inside.

Once we started driving, I told him about Ethan and what I'd seen. "You can't stay here," I finished. "It's too dangerous."

"We already knew someone was hunting merrow," he said. "How does this change anything?"

"Because Ethan goes to *our school*. He brought that knife with him for a reason. If he doesn't already know what you are, he suspects something."

"If that's true, and it probably is, you're not safe either. I'm not leaving you here alone with him."

I frowned and crossed my arms. After seeing how powerful and fast Sebastian was, I couldn't imagine any human actually hurting him. But that didn't mean he should be reckless, or put himself in harm's way.

"You're cute when you pout," Sebastian laughed, glancing over at me. "Fine, I won't go to school anymore. I was thinking of dropping out anyway. Happy?" he asked.

I bit my lip, but nodded. It did make me feel a little better, and I hadn't really wanted Sebastian to leave. And for some reason, riding with him, I just couldn't stay scared. There were things to be afraid of, sure. But there was also so much to be excited about. Like learning to swim, *so I could become a freaking mermaid.*

At first I'd suggested a bathtub filled with salt water, but Sebastian said it wasn't the same as real sea water. Plus we both needed to fit in it. The trouble was finding a place that was free from spectators. He suggested swimming at night, when it was dark, which seemed particularly stupid to me. There were stretches of beaches between the cliffs that were only accessible by boat—I wasn't keen on that idea. Plus I was adamant about starting out in shallow water, not more than two feet.

"Where are we going?" I asked, as Sebastian pulled into the parking area for Dunluce castle. *We're going to swim here?* Sebastian turned off the car and we got out.

"It's closed," I said, nodding to the sign.

Opening hours, 10am to 4pm

"Perfect, no tourists." He grinned and grabbed my hand, pulling me forward. The sky was cerulean blue with a scattering of puffy white clouds; it contrasted perfectly with the yellow-green grass covering the ground, and the crumbling ruins, which were orange-gray, and cast dramatic shadows in the late afternoon light. The gates leading to the narrow bridge were closed and locked with a heavy chain, but Sebastian lowered himself down over the ledge to a small path below. Then he turned back and held out his arms to help me down.

I hesitated, but then reached out to him. His hands ran up the sides of my body as I slid down, and he caught me by the arms when I landed. The ancient castle walls loomed above us, the vacant spaces where the windows and doors used to be watched us trespass. We followed the trail until we were directly under the bridge, which was supported by a stone archway. We could see the ocean on both sides of the historical site. Then there were wooden steps leading to the right, around the castle. The walls narrowed until we were in a deep ravine, and the path dropped steeply until the sheer basalt cliffs stretched hundreds of feet above us.

My jaw dropped open when we reached the end of the trail and were confronted with the entrance of a wide cavern. It cut straight through the rock beneath the castle; I could see the ocean and sky on the other side, the clouds now turning pink over the sparkling blue water. A sign announced our destination.

MERMAID'S CAVE

"Shut up," I said, putting my hands on my hips. "Seriously?"

Sebastian grinned back at me, then stepped through the opening into the cave. Inside it was like an underground cathedral. The ceiling was a wide arch, and the hole leading out to the ocean was narrower at the base, almost like a keyhole. Ocean water flowed deep into the cave, where it reflected the sky, and cast a blue and purple shimmer over the stone ceiling.

We walked over the large, smooth rocks, until we reached the shallow pool, which was directly below the castle. I could sense the weight of thousands of tons of rocks on top of us.

"At high tide, the area can be dangerous," Sebastian said, "but at low tide..." he gestured in front of him. The water was perfectly still, cut off from the choppy ocean waves. There was plenty of light coming through the mouth of the cave, infusing the water with remarkable clarity.

"It's amazing," I said.

Sebastian took off his shirt and tossed it aside, then unbuckled his belt. I turned away, blushing.

"Relax, I'll keep my briefs on... this time."

He was wearing a European-style speedo. I tried not to stare at his ass as he waded into the natural pool. At its center, the water just barely reached his knees. Sebastian's muscular body was framed by the mouth of the cave, his silhouette outlined by the turquoise sea behind him. His torso was perfectly reflected in the cave's mirror-like pool, and I could see the colorful sparkling as the salt water interacted with his skin. It was so beautiful, I could hardly breathe.

"See? Nothing to it." He splashed a little water in my direction, before falling back into the water, submerging himself. When he stood up again, his whole body was sparkling like he'd been powdered in fairy dust.

I almost asked him to turn around before I took off my shirt and pants, but it wasn't like I was getting naked—I had a suit on. I put my clothes in a corner of the cave next to some larger rocks, then walked into the water carefully. As the cold water lapped over my ankles, I got goose pimples and rubbed my arms. The rocks were slippery, and I held out my hands for balance as I waded deeper. When I got closer to Sebastian, I gasped.

His skin was already starting to change. It grew harder, and flakey, with hundreds of shimmering scales. The exo spread up over his stomach and sides, though it was much thinner and smoother here, like a snakeskin. I ran my hands over the side of his body, feeling the texture and toughness. Then he lay back in the water again, and I watched the exo grow over his upper body and shoulders.

A tail was forming around his legs, binding them together in segments, like body armor. It looked like a lobster tail, but much more colorful: greenish purple, with patches of bright turquoise, flaring into burning orange at its tips.

But the coolest thing were his hands. His long, sensitive fingers gleamed like polished shells. It looked like he was wearing lightweight boxing gloves of some kind, with the flat front.

I reached for his hand—his fingers felt like giant crab legs, the kind you need a special metal tool to crack open. "Your turn," he said, still holding my hand. He pulled me gently down into the water and held my shoulders as I leaned back.

"Don't worry, I've got you. You don't even need to go underwater right now, not yet. Just lean back and try to relax."

I lay back in the water and felt my skin tingle; I could see the lights and colors as the sea water met my skin. But when I lifted my feet up I panicked, kicking up and accidentally throwing my head back into the water. I was sure I was going to suck in a huge gulp of saltwater, but Sebastian caught me and held me up.

"Just breathe deeply. Take more air into your lungs. With your lungs full, you can't sink."

I took a deep breath and held the air in... it seemed to work. I closed my eyes and tried to relax, concentrating on my breathing. My body bobbed up and down in the water with each breath, as my lungs increased my buoyancy. I learned to keep enough air in my lungs so that my ears stayed above the surface. I could hear the wind rushing through the mouth of the cave and the surf beating outside. It was peaceful.

When I opened my eyes again, the cave was on fire. Everything glowed, like pink and orange flames were climbing the walls. The pool danced and sparkled with colors and lights I couldn't even begin to describe. I thought I was on drugs, or hallucinating.

I saw Sebastian sitting on a rock a few feet away and panicked again, realizing he was no longer holding me up. I flailed my arms and pushed my hands down into the water to stabilize myself. My fingers dragged slowly through the water, with more resistance than I expected. I lifted one hand up in front of my face and saw it had formed a bit of webbing between each finger, like a frog. *That's new.*

"My vision is funny," I said, sitting up.

"We have more color receptors than humans do. Humans have three primary colors. Butterflies have five. We have sixteen. It comes in handy when we're deep in the sea, beyond light, where everything looks black. You probably aren't seeing that many colors yet, but it's a good sign."

"How come my exo isn't like yours?" I asked, running my fingertips over my skin. It was tougher now, and smooth like eggshells.

"That's not your exo, that's just a base reaction. First you'll need to have your metamorphosis, and then grow and regrow several exos before you get one like mine."

Metamorphosis. Like a butterfly. Unless I couldn't change. I tried not to think of what that would mean for Sebastian and me. I held my legs together tightly, willing them to bind together the way Sebastian's had. I held the pose for several minutes, but nothing else happened. It was anticlimactic. I smiled and shrugged at Sebastian, trying to keep the disappointment off my face. *No tail. Now what?*

Sebastian crossed to the other end of the pool. "Try swimming over to me," he said. "The trick is, don't breathe under water— you won't be able to do that until you can turn completely.

Breathe out when you're underwater, or hold your breath. Breathe in when your head lifts up." He showed me what he meant, miming long breast strokes and breathing in when his head came up to the side.

I wasn't so sure about that. Instead, I paddled over to him, keeping my mouth and nose above the water. I used my webbed fingers to pull myself forward and let my legs dangle behind me. My knees bumped against the rocks on the bottom of the shallow pool, but it didn't hurt as much as I expected it to. The pain felt distant somehow, like I was wearing a layer of cardboard over my skin.

When I reached him, I stood up too quickly and toppled over the slippery rocks. He caught me and we tumbled to the ground, our wet arms entwined. He laughed and squeezed me against him. I felt the hard edges of his exo pressing into me, but not painfully. We gazed into each other's eyes, inches apart. I licked my lips, sure he was going to kiss me this time. But then he broke eye contact, and shifted to increase the distance between us.

"Sorry," he mumbled, looking away.

"It's fine, I get it," I said, though I didn't really. He said we couldn't have sex, but that didn't mean we couldn't kiss. He'd already broken the rules, right? *Maybe he's not attracted to me.*

His face darkened and he pushed his wet hair out of his face. "I want to be with you," he said, "but there's still so much you don't know."

"So tell me," I said, crossly this time. "I thought we were done with secrets."

"Even if you can change, you might not like it down there. You're imagining a fairy tale, but not all merrow are like me. We can be dangerous. Ruthless."

"Um, I know. Bedelia, remember?"

"It's not just that," he said, sighing. He looked out at the ocean for a moment, before continuing. "In the beginning, merrow would come up on land often. We enjoyed living in the sun, and the way humans treated us. We would take lovers, maybe start families. We'd give them some of our blood when they were sick, to make them live longer, to keep them strong and healthy. Because of ecdysis, our blood can heal human injuries as well. These people, our human families, were the Tuatha Dé."

I nodded. I'd guessed as much, or close to it. Why was he telling me this now?

"But they got greedy. They discovered other uses for our blood, besides healing—what you would call magic. First came the contests, with humans competing in magical feats for increased status or wealth. Then, the families started fighting with each other, using magic as a weapon."

"They needed more blood," I guessed.

"A lot more. The Tuatha Dé were insatiable. They started hunting merrow; building special nets and traps. During the worst of it, there were farms. Merrow were forced to breed in captivity and then slaughtered like cattle. Drained for their blood."

"Oh my god," I said, holding a hand up to my mouth. The sun was setting and the cave was chilly. My upper body had dried off, and my hands and skin returned to normal. I felt a shiver run up my spine and crossed my arms.

"When the royal family discovered what was happening, they nearly destroyed the Tuatha Dé. Then they demanded sacrifices to keep the human population under control. Some Fomori treated the humans like slaves, considering themselves a superior race. Until the day a half-blood led a revolution. First he disabled our most powerful weapon, which backfired and decimated the Fomorian army. Then he beheaded the Fomorian general."

"Lugh. The general was his own grandfather, Balor."

Sebastian looked at me with a dumbstruck expression.

"How the hell—"

"I read a lot," I smiled coyly.

"Nerd," he teased. I splashed water at his face, and he wiped it away with his hand.

"When the Tuatha Dé won, the royal family made it illegal for merrow to breed with humans, or to reveal themselves. We moved down into the deepest oceans, and became things of folklore and legend. For a while, we lived openly in Iceland, and later in Florida, but in time, those became overrun with humans as well. In the last few centuries, the merrow returned to the deep seas, and built underwater cities with new technology. There are only about a hundred thousand of us left."

"But all that stuff happened a long time ago, right? The wars between the Tuatha Dé and the merrow."

Sebastian nodded. "Thousands of years ago."

"So what does any of that have to do with us?"

"Merrow have long memories. And remember, we live longer. So while most humans have forgotten the brutality and injustice that led to the merrow wars, the older merrow are still angry. They hate *all* humans. And now that the royal family is missing...

some merrow think it's time to stop hiding. They argue that the humans are destroying the world, and that it's our duty to wipe them out."

"Wait—*what?*" He'd said the last statement so casually, I almost didn't grasp its significance. "There are merrow who want to destroy the human race?" I pictured a hundred thousand Sebastians, capable of punching through picnic tables and moving faster than we could even see them. It would be a slaughter. A mermaid apocalypse. I almost laughed at the thought, but the impulse died in my throat. I felt sick. I couldn't believe I'd wanted to kiss him just a few moments ago.

"I don't want that, of course, but some of my family—"

"Your family wants to destroy the human race? How could they even consider something like that?"

"It's not like they have much of a choice. Humans have been dumping toxic waste into the oceans for decades, it's getting worse all the time. Species that have been around for thousands of years are going extinct by the hundreds. If we stay hidden and do nothing, we'll all die."

"Oh my god. You *agree* with them." I pulled away from him, horrified.

"I don't agree with them, I just *understand* them. Should we just wait for the humans to accidentally exterminate us by destroying the oceans? Or should we do something about it? There isn't a simple solution."

Sebastian was right. I had been imagining a fairy tale ending, where we would swim off together into the sunset. But those visions were shattered now. Even if I could change fully, I'd never belong with the merrow. I thought of Derry and Jackie. All my new friends here in Ireland, and all the old ones back in America. Sure, maybe we didn't recycle as much as we should, but that wasn't our fault. We weren't evil. We didn't deserve to be wiped off the face of the planet. But if the merrow did attack, what could we do to stop them? *Absolutely nothing.*

22

At school the next day, I was greeted by a bouquet of irises in front of my locker. There was no card, but I assumed they were from Sebastian. *Sorry my race wants to destroy your race.* I was about to pick them up when I saw Travis hovering a few feet away. Why would Travis give me flowers?

"Like them?" he asked, smiling.

We'd had virtually no interaction since the first day of school. Why do flowers always come from someone who's done something wrong, or someone you have no feelings for? Actually, I realized, this was the first time I'd gotten flowers from a boy. Ever.

"Yeah," I said, breathing in the musky floral scent. "They're beautiful."

"I noticed you looked kind of sad today," he said. "So I just thought, you know, *flowers.*"

I hoped everybody at school wasn't as observant as Travis. After Sebastian's stunt on the hurley field, a lot of the guys in school were treating him like a rock star, and the girls had been swooning since day one. I was no troll myself; I'd almost started *expecting* the attention I received for my looks. But with people watching my every move, I'd have to be extra careful.

Travis was still standing there with a stupid grin on his face. I wondered what he thought would happen next. We'd make out? I'd realize he was the one for me?

"This is really sweet of you, Travis. Thanks. I've just been, really busy with homework recently, I'm way behind, so I've been staying up studying. I guess I'm just tired, I didn't realize anybody could see it." That wasn't even a lie. All the teachers had gone easy with me for the first week, but now they expected me to finish work on time, and they were tough. I got my first ever 'D' in Miss Lynch's class. A few months ago, that would have been grounds for a major meltdown. Now it barely registered. Compared to the news I'd received yesterday concerning the potential end of mankind, a bad grade on my report card didn't seem like such a big deal.

"Anyway, thanks for trying to cheer me up. It worked." I smiled at him, stretching my lips as far as they would go before it turned into a grimace. Then I stuffed the flowers in my locker and headed to class.

I'd just sat down and pulled out my binder and a pencil, when I heard the whispers about another dead girl. Not from our school this time; about an hour south of here. But she'd been drowned and lain out on the beach, just like Bedelia. The police were talking about a serial killer. She was found yesterday afternoon, which meant she'd been drowning in one part of the ocean while I was learning to swim in another. Thinking about it made my skin crawl. It didn't make me *responsible*, exactly, but I couldn't escape feeling guilty. After all, nobody else even knew what they were looking for, besides Sebastian and I.

And unless we did something about it, I realized, the bodies were going to keep coming. And by *we*, I meant Sebastian. What could I possibly do against another merrow? They were a hundred times faster and stronger than I could ever be. I'd only get in the way. But would Sebastian really go against his own kind to save some humans? And what did I expect him to do, find the merrow and kill him? I thought about my own near-death experience on the pier, and the engraved dagger that had tasted my blood. Was I prepared to inflict that kind of pain; to *end* a life? Plus, there was no guarantee Sebastian would even be able to defeat another merrow one-on-one. What if he got hurt, or killed? I wasn't willing to risk that. We needed help, and I thought I knew where to get it.

According to Ethan, The Tuatha Dé had been able to defeat the Fomorians because they were using Fomorian blood. *Merrow* blood. Although the thought made me sick to my stomach, and what Sebastian had told me about the Tuatha Dé's breeding farms horrified me, right then I knew two things: The Tuatha Dé had successfully defeated a Fomorian army in the past, and if what I'd seen Ethan do was any indication, they were still around.

When I finally saw Ethan in the hall after second period, I made a beeline for him. I was planning to demand he listen to me, and had organized arguments in my head to overcome his objections. So I was surprised when he grabbed my wrist and whispered, "We need to talk."

He dragged me to the nearest exit and pushed me outside. Did he know what I was? Was the dagger still in his backpack? I considered screaming as he led me around behind the school. He shoved me down onto the bench in front of the old chapel, then sat down next to me. He took a deep breath, looked me in the eyes, and said, "Sebastian is going to kill you."

He said it like a confession. Like a secret. For a second, I wondered if he knew something I didn't. But Sebastian wouldn't hurt me.

"He killed Bedelia," Ethan continued. "And the other girl, the one they found yesterday."

I frowned. "No, he didn't. He was with me, Jackie and Derry the day Bedelia was killed. And he was with me all day yesterday. He couldn't have done it."

"Then he had help," Ethan said. "But trust me, he knows who is responsible." I couldn't argue with him on that point, so I changed the subject.

"On my second night here, someone put a note on my door," I said, reaching into my bag. I'd pressed the scrap of parchment in a book. As I passed it to him our fingers brushed together and I felt a warmth, like an electrical current, pass between us. Ethan pulled his hand back suddenly—he'd felt it too. He studied the note; his lips moving as he mouthed the words silently. Then his eyebrows furled together in confusion.

"This doesn't make any sense. You found this on your door?" he asked.

"Yes," I said, my hands folded in my lap. Ethan was already agitated, and I needed him to calm down so he'd open up to me. I wasn't sure I wanted to try soothing his emotions. For the moment he seemed to be trying to protect me, rather than kill me—I didn't want to press my luck.

"Why are you showing this to me?" Ethan asked.

"Because I think you know what it means," I said.

Ethan ran his fingers through his hair, and a gust of wind blew a handful of leaves over our shoes.

"Look, I know you don't owe me anything," I pushed, "but I have a feeling I'm in danger. If that note is a threat, I need to find out who wants to hurt me."

"It's not a threat," Ethan said, tracing the script with the tip of his finger. "I don't think. More like a protective ward. But are you sure it was even for you? It doesn't have your name on it. I mean, no offense but you're new here. You haven't had much time to make enemies."

"I think it has something to do with my mother."

I pulled out the photograph of my mom and her friends.

"Do you recognize this boy? His name was Colin Blake, he was friends with my mother."

Ethan took the picture, his eyes widening.

"Um, yeah. That's my uncle."

I squeezed my eyes together.

What?

He reached into his bag, and I tensed on the edge of my seat. He wouldn't stab me at school, in broad daylight, would he? I breathed a sigh of relief when he pulled out his school binder instead, and held it up for me. His name was written across the front.

Ethan Blake.

23

"Your mother was Branna Daly?" Ethan said, standing up and clenching his fists. "Holy shit." We stared at each other in silence for a moment. It was like we were seeing each other for the first time.

"The weird thing is, I didn't even know her real name until a month ago; she moved to America when she was sixteen and used a fake name, Branna Bishop. Then she married my dad and became Branna Clark. I've been Clara Clark my whole life, and now I'm suddenly in Ireland pulling skeletons out of closets."

"And that's not just a metaphor. My uncle Colin was murdered," Ethan said.

"Yeah," I nodded. "From what I can tell, the same night my mom fled the country."

A flash of anger crossed Ethan's face, and I realized again how much he looked like the man I saw in the pub.

"I hope you're not saying your mom killed my uncle," he said.

"I don't think so," I said, shaking my head. "I think someone was after my mom. Maybe the same person who killed your uncle. But if that note was meant to protect me, then somebody else knows what really happened, and thinks I'm in danger. Look, I have no idea what's going on, and I'm obviously in way over my head. I need some answers."

"About what?" he said.

"For starters... how you pushed Brody that far back. Or how you make other things move around. I've seen your tattoos flash, they burn like embers when you're doing something unnatural."

His eyes darkened, "You don't know what you're talking about." He started walking away, and I followed behind him.

"Come on, I've seen it. I know it's real, I just want to know how it works."

We walked further away from the building, into an area of the grounds I hadn't been to before. The small path led between some trees to a narrow gravel road, lined with sprawling beech trees. Their intersecting limbs stretched over the road to make an archway. Ethan stopped walking in the middle of the road, which was completely empty in both directions. He looked sullen, and when he opened his brooding mouth, I was afraid he was going to lie again. Instead he leaned in and said, "We aren't allowed to talk about it."

"How about if I guess?" I asked.

"No offense," he smirked, "but I don't think you're that creative."

I bit my lip. I'd have to choose my words carefully, or else Ethan would ask where my knowledge came from. "You said, in the library, that Lugh could only defeat the Fomori because he had Fomori blood in him. Lugh's people were the Tuatha Dé, descendants of the Fomori. But each new generation would have *less* Fomori blood in them, making them weaker."

Ethan crossed his arms, looking nervous.

"So I *surmise*," I continued, "that the Tuatha Dé found a way to get more blood from the Fomorians, and use it somehow." I reached over and pushed up his sleeve to reveal the large tattoo covering his upper arm and shoulder. As my fingertips touched his bicep, I felt the strange buzz of electricity again. For the first time, I realized the tattoo was a pair of dragons, bound together in a complex Celtic knot, with symbols hidden throughout the design. It was outlined in black, but the middle of each line was red. *Blood* red.

"Oh, and the Fomorians are merrow—mermaids. Half fish, half human. Did I miss anything?"

Ethan stared at me, too stunned to speak. Then he pulled his sleeve back down and grunted approvingly. "You know, you're a lot smarter than you look."

"Thanks *a lot*." I rolled my eyes.

"I didn't mean—I just meant, you know, beautiful girls aren't always known for their brains," he said, looking embarrassed. I was suddenly very aware of how alone we were. Alone, together.

Is that why he drew that picture of me? He thinks I'm beautiful? *Focus.*

"Anyway, now you can't get in trouble, right? You're not telling me anything I didn't already know. You're just filling in the details."

He sighed, "I guess that makes sense. Though, you basically just admitted to believing in mermaids, so if you tell anybody else any of this they're going to lock you up."

"Mutually ensured destruction then," I said, holding up my little finger. We pinkie-shook on it.

He ran his hand through his long, dark hair, and I caught a whiff of woodchips and musk. I was getting to like the smell of him. I wondered what his house smelled like. We started walking down the road, looping around to the front of the school. It was strange how comfortable I felt with Ethan. I didn't really trust him, and I was pretty sure he'd hate me if he found out what I was. But I felt like I could be myself around him.

"In my family," Ethan said finally, "we talk a lot about the old tales. And we know there is more to the world than most people accept."

"Like magic," I said.

"Kind of, though we call it the craft. It's old magic, but you're right, it works by merrow blood."

"Can you tell me the history? From the beginning?"

"I can try," he said. "But not here. How do you feel about a field trip?"

We'd reached the front of the school. I was prepared to go back in, but Ethan nodded towards the parking lot.

"It's not even lunch yet, and you want me to leave school?" I asked.

"There's a place I think you should see. It'll help you understand. I can have us back before school's out."

Ethan walked over to his bike and pulled a spare helmet out of the seat. I hesitated before taking it. What would Sebastian think about me leaving school with Ethan, when I already knew he had a knife matching the one my attacker had used? What would *my mother* have thought about me jumping on the back of some guy's motorcycle? But I couldn't just go back inside and pretend to be a normal high school kid anymore. We had to find out who was killing girls my age, and then we had to stop them. If Ethan had answers, I needed to hear them. But that didn't mean I had to be reckless.

"Let me just tell Jackie and Derry I'm with you," I said, pulling out my phone. I scanned his face for a reaction, but he made no move to stop me. If he was planning on killing me, he wouldn't want anybody else to know we were together, right? I sent them both the same message.

Left school for a while
with Ethan
text you later

At least now someone would know where to look for my body. I put the phone back in my pocket and strapped on the helmet. The first five minutes on the bike were exhilarating. I wrapped my arms around Ethan's waist as we flew down narrow country roads, weaving between the grass-covered hills, my dark hair streaming in the wind like a kite. Twenty minutes later, my butt was asleep from the vibration, and my arms were getting sore from holding on. But it was worth it when we reached our destination.

"Welcome to Beaghmore," Ethan said, after dismounting and helping me off the bike. We parked on the top of a small hill and I could see the site spread out before us—large stones stood straight up in a haphazard pattern. From what I could see, there were three rings of stones and one lone circle, which had hundreds of small pointed stones set into the ground inside a stone ring. Some of the standing stones were as tall as I was. Nearby was a large pile of rocks, surrounded by a wide depression, and then a ditch. It looked like a UFO had landed. The lawn around the stones was bright green and carefully trimmed, but it was unnatural. Where we were standing, the ground was dry, with tall yellow weeds.

"What's that?" I pointed to the pile of rocks.

"Supposedly, a burial mound—a cairn."

"But actually..." I prompted.

"I don't know how much of this is true," Ethan said, sitting on a nearby boulder. "This is just the story I was told."

I nodded for him to continue.

"In the old days, so the legends go, the merrow came and taught humans technology. They taught us magic, how to use their blood. We were never sick, never hungry, never in pain. When the Fomorians were family, we had an unlimited supply of merrow blood. We were nearly as strong as they were, and we lived almost as long. But humans became dependent on it. More blood and we could survive any battle. More blood and we could outlive our enemies. Those who could get enough of it formed powerful dynasties. After a few decades of slaughtering each other, only twelve families remained."

"This was the Tuatha Dé Danann: circle builders and metal workers, with Druidic arts and new, magical technology. They combined metallurgy and merrow blood magic to produce four powerful talismans. The Stone of Destiny, which would roar when the rightful king was inaugurated; The Spear of Lugh, which would always ensure victory; The Sword of Nuadha, from which no-one could escape; and The Cauldron of the Daghdha, from which no-one would go away unsatisfied. Every three branches of the Tuatha Dé formed one clan, and was given one of the talismans for safekeeping. This ensured they'd never go to war against each other."

Ethan lifted up his sleeve and showed me a tattoo on his wrist. It was small and looked like a family crest. Close up, I could see it had the design of a spear in the center.

"You're a *descendant* of Lugh?" I asked, with a sharp intake of breath.

"That's the story anyway. It was a long time ago, and sometimes I wonder if the families just made up their heritage. I mean, we have legends about the talismans, great feats of magic and power—but I've never seen them. Powerful artifacts like that were literally fueled by merrow blood. They drank it like a car drinks gasoline."

"That's when the merrow began to disappear," I said, the stories starting to come together in my mind.

Ethan nodded. "When they left, our way of life was destroyed. We learned how to conserve the blood, channel it, and focus it. But even so, the blood was scarce. Soon it was a hundred times more valuable than gold. Fishermen who could catch a merrow child could earn a whole year's wages."

I nodded. Sebastian had already told me most of this.

"The merrow reciprocated. They'd come on land and charm all the children into the ocean with their music. That's where the pied piper story really comes from—they could make humans do just about anything. Sometimes they'd make a whole town march to the cliffs and throw themselves into the sea. Those are the old stories, anyway."

Sebastian hadn't told me that part.

"And the magic? How does it work?" I asked.

"It's not like the magic you see in movies; making an elephant appear or disappear. It's more like sympathetic magic. You know, *like attracts like.*"

He pulled a small stone from his pocket and held it up. With the light behind it, I could see it was dark blue. "The Fomori who came on land used these: they called them Bætulia, or contriving stones. They were supposed to fall from heaven."

He held it over his motorcycle keys, and I saw them move.

"It's a magnet!" I said.

"Kind of, but not as limited. Merrow blood is magnetically charged, because they live so deep in the ocean, closer to the earth's crust. Their blood is full of minerals and metals; including some very trace elements that don't seem to exist anywhere else. It reacts to the Bætulia in unique ways. A drop of merrow blood on a ten-ton boulder, for example, and we can use Bætulia to lift it up. That's how Beaghmore and other megaliths were made. The merrow did it themselves, at first, to mark their territory."

"And the tattoos?" I prompted.

"The tattoos are made from special ink, a mix of merrow blood and powdered Bætulia. The combination is like stored up gunpowder; I can draw on it when I need it, activating it with some special words or incantations, focusing my attention, drawing the energy to other parts of my body."

He pulled up his shirt to show me more of the tattoo, a trail of runes and symbols that went from his neck down to his chiseled abdomen.

"Show me," I said, hungry for knowledge.

Ethan grinned and took his shirt off. The double dragons wrapped around his neck and shoulders, crossing several times across his back, with the tails disappearing under the top of Ethan's pants. His chest was smooth and muscular. I felt my cheeks grow warm.

"The tattoos store energy, but it's limited. If I pick up a small stone or object, it costs me a little. If I throw it with force, it costs more. It's usually more efficient to direct the energy inward, to speed up my movement, my reactions, my strength."

"That's what you did to Brody?" I asked.

"Yes. But, I don't have enough ink in me to lift one of these big stones. It would take several of us together to move it. And even then, we can only lift our own weight; unless we also put a drop of blood on the stone itself, which boosts the effects. This," he said, "was a training ground. Most of these stones were smeared with merrow blood, a long, long time ago, which makes it easier for me to lift them."

Ethan reached out a hand towards the circle full of small stones, and I saw them tremble in the ground like little gophers pushing up dirt. "But like I said, merrow blood is precious. It would be wasteful to use it just to show off for a girl," he said, smirking. "Plus there are much cooler things we can do, that don't take as much energy."

He walked over to a bush and grabbed a handful of leaves, then threw them up in the air. He held his hands out like he was trying to shoot lighting from his fingertips and whispered some words I didn't understand. I saw one of the symbols in his tattoo flare up and heard a hissing noise. Instead of falling, the leaves floated higher, coming together in pairs. When each had a partner, they flapped around like butterflies. I clapped my hands as they spun around us. One of them landed on my arm, then took off again.

"Drumroll, please," Ethan said. I slapped my hands against my thighs to make a rhythm. He brought his arm down sharply, and all the leaves burst into flame, turning into a cloud of sparks and burning embers. They floated in the air around us like fireflies, darting between the ancient standing stones, before winking out one by one.

"That was incredible," I said, tossing Ethan his shirt.

"But like I said, I don't know what's actually true. Our family has a few bottles of the magic potion in our cellar, but I've never entirely believed it was mermaid blood. I thought those were just stories for children. I figured it might be something else that science just didn't understand yet. Some kind of special space lava."

"Space lava?" I cocked an eyebrow at him.

He grinned and shrugged his shoulders, "All I'm saying is, I've never really believed in the whole 'mermaid' thing, until recently." Alarm bells sounded in my head. *He knows.*

"I knew they were real after Bedelia died. That's something they used to do, a long time ago. You've got to understand, they're natural born killers. The Tuatha Dé, we're *defending* humanity," he said, walking over to his bike. I held my breath as he unzipped his backpack and pulled out the antique dagger. I was right. It was identical to the one that I'd seen my attacker use. Ethan held it up in front of me and I flinched away from the sharp blade.

"A family heirloom," he said. "My father gave it to me when I turned thirteen. He told me about our history, and about the merrow." Ethan ran his finger down the length of the engraved blade. "The blood gets caught in these grooves, then flows into the handle, which is hollow. It can store three ounces of blood." Ethan said all this with pride, as if he were at show and tell. I tried to keep the look of horror off my face.

"What are you going to use it for?" I asked, dreading the response.

"My father also told me that a merrow killed his brother, Colin. He said if I ever met one, I should plunge this into their abdomen, and twist," Ethan said, clenching the knife, with a bitter look on his face.

My heart was pounding as I searched Ethan's dark eyes for suspicion. Did he know that my mother was half merrow, that *I* was part merrow? My fingers curled around a small stone. I wondered if I'd be fast enough to use it. The pause seemed to stretch forever, but finally Ethan relaxed his grip on the knife and leaned back against the rock behind him.

"Sebastian is one of them," he said, with hatred in his eyes. "And I'm going to kill him."

24

I should have feigned surprise, but instead my face lit up with relief that I wasn't on the receiving end of the dagger. By the time I thought about denying it, or lying, Ethan had seen the truth.

"You already know," his eyes widened.

"He told me a few days ago," I said.

"You *know* he isn't human—and you're still into him? You're dating a monster." He wrinkled his nose in disgust.

"I'm not sure if we're technically *dating*..." I said.

Ethan held up his palm and cut me off.

"Merrow are dangerous, and you're seriously deluded if you think he cares about you. He's using his powers over you, to seduce you. That's what they do. You can't help being attracted to him, but it isn't real."

His words stung. I was about to start yelling at him, but I caught myself. What was I going to say, that he was wrong? I *was* attracted to Sebastian, even drawn to him. I couldn't stop thinking about him when he wasn't with me. But I didn't feel *coerced*. I didn't get all doe-eyed and silly like most other girls did in his presence.

But how would I know if Sebastian was using his merrow powers on me? Was my attraction just a trick? However they got there, I *did* have feelings for Sebastian. Deep feelings, that hit me in ways I'd never felt before. In that moment, I realized it was foolish to be angry at Sebastian because some crazy merrow wanted to rid the world of humans. It wasn't his fault. I looked down at the gleaming blade in Ethan's hand. The thought of it being used on Sebastian made me sick to my stomach.

I would not let that happen. If Ethan liked me, even a little, maybe I could change his mind.

"You're right," I said finally. "There is a merrow in town killing girls, and we have to stop him."

I put my fingers on his arm and made him look at me. "But it's not Sebastian."

Ethan scowled and pulled his arm away.

"He's got some kind of spell over you," he said.

"Sebastian is *helping* me find the real killer," I said. "He's just as angry about it as you are."

Ethan shrugged. "I doubt that's true, and it doesn't make him innocent."

"You can't kill him," I said, a plea in my voice.

"Even if I don't," he said, crossing his arms, "he won't last another week up here. Merrow blood is extremely valuable to the Tuatha Dé, remember?"

My blood ran cold as I pictured Sebastian's broken body on the pile of rocks nearby, his blood collected and then used to tattoo the flesh of the Tuatha Dé. The scene around us no longer seemed as mystical or beautiful as it had when we arrived at Beaghmore. The sun had lowered in the horizon, and now the stones cast long shadows that stretched like menacing fingers across the too-green grass. The longer Sebastian stayed on land, the more danger he was in. Even if Ethan didn't kill him, someone else would. My chest tightened, making it hard to breathe.

"You can't tell anyone," I said, grabbing Ethan's arm. "Your people would kill him."

"Without a doubt. And they'd kill each other just to get at him." Ethan clenched his jaw. He wasn't going to listen to me. I had to buy time.

"Give me a month," I begged, closing the distance between us until I could feel his warm breath on my cheeks. "Sebastian will find the other merrow, and we'll deliver him to you. You'll still be the hero. You'll still bring a body back to your family, filled with more merrow blood than they've ever seen. Everybody wins." *What am I saying?*

"And if he doesn't?" Ethan asked.

"Then I'll help you kill him."

***

Yesterday, I thought there was no hope for the human race against an army of merrow. But after watching Ethan, I wasn't so sure. How could you pick a winning team if both sides could do things you've never dreamed of? Unfortunately for me, I was part merrow… which meant, if Ethan knew what I really was, he'd probably want to kill me too. At least I'd bought Sebastian some time. We just had to find the real killer, and quickly.

I'd missed the bus, so Ethan dropped me off at home. There was a white van parked out front that I didn't recognize. I let myself in, and saw Aedan sitting on the couch with a woman leaning over him. At first I thought I was interrupting something illicit, but then I saw the long white cast propped up on a chair.

"What happened?" I asked.

"Just bad luck," he said. "Was up on a ladder painting the rims and somehow the ladder slipped away from me. I fell, snapped my leg."

My mood, which was already low, sank through the floor. I felt crushed under the weight of Aedan's emotions. He was angry at himself for falling and scared about not being able to work until his leg healed. He'd always looked so upbeat and positive, but I realized now he must have been making an effort. *For me.* He looked so old and fragile now, and behind his false smile there was a weakness and dejection that had been festering for decades—probably since my mother left. I felt bad that I'd never really asked him about work. I'd been too preoccupied with my own problems.

"This is Helena," he said, fidgeting a little. "She works at the hospital."

Helena was pretty, with blond hair streaked with silver, and busty. The tight white cardigan buttoned at the waist was straining to contain her as she leaned over Aedan.

"Aye, had a right old spill," she said, wiping his chin with a napkin. She'd been feeding him a bowl of soup and was still holding the spoon. "Shouldn't be working at all, at his age."

"Houses ain't going to paint themselves," said Aedan. He was worrying about paying the bills, I realized. I didn't know money was a problem; I'd assumed he could access the money my parents left me. Was he paying for everything out of his own pocket? My new clothes, the phone bill?

"I need to get back to work," Helena said, "but you keep him off his feet. He shouldn't put any weight on it for at least a month."

"Not going to happen," Aedan said with a frown. "I've got to finish the Boyle's house this weekend. If I don't get it done they'll find someone else."

"Can we help?" I asked.

"I couldn't ask you to do that," he said. "You've got school to worry about." I smiled. If school was my biggest concern, I'd be in heaven.

"I've painted rooms in our house before, back home. I could get a couple of my friends together and do it. You could teach us how, and supervise the work. It'd be fun."

"That sounds like a fine offer," Helena said. "At your age, you'll be lucky if this heals right and you don't have to use a cane for the rest of your life. Seriously. Bed rest. Stay in. Watch old movies."

"Maybe if you come watch them with me," Aedan said, but then looked surprised at his boldness and his cheeks turned red.

"My Lord, Aedan Daly, are you asking me on a date? You should be ashamed of yourself," but she smiled and pinched his cheek. "Just kidding, handsome. Give me a ring anytime."

It wasn't until I reached my room and pulled my mom's phone out of my backpack that I noticed I had several missed calls, and half a dozen text messages from Sebastian.

Swimming after school?

I need to see you

We have more to discuss

Let me know when you're ready to talk

Jackie says you left school with Ethan

WHERE ARE YOU?!

I texted back quickly.

I'm fine

Come over tonight, 11pm

I'll open the window

I paused, then added,

Need to see you too

That night I asked Aedan if he had any family albums, with pictures of my mother as a child, and Phyllis. Now that I knew I was part merrow, I had even more questions about my mother and grandmother. If marrying humans was forbidden, why did Phyllis live on land? Did she fall in love, or was she running away from something. Sebastian said the older merrow were even more hateful of the humans... so why did my grandmother marry one?

"Met her on the beach one day and asked her to marry me," Aedan said, pulling a pair of heavy albums from drawer.

"How romantic," I said. I knew there must be more to that story, but how could I ask Aedan without giving away my secret, and potentially putting him in danger? Besides, he looked exhausted. He had difficulty moving around the small room with his cast, so I helped him into his room so he could get some sleep.

Miscreant sank into the sofa next to me, purring as I flipped through the album and held photos up to the lamp in the living room. I'd seen pictures of my grandmother before; my mom kept a framed portrait of her in her bedroom, even though she never talked about her. But I was seeing her in a whole new light now. In her childhood photos, my mother looked happier than I'd ever seen her—an adorable little girl with wide eyes and dirty knees.

Looking at the pictures of my mother brought my grief rushing back to me. My eyes watered up and I brushed away a tear. I missed her so much sometimes, I could hardly breathe. Phyllis, in contrast, brought up no such emotions. She was so glamorous, looking at photos of her was like flipping through a magazine. She didn't even seem real. I looked closer and saw that she wore the same necklace in most of the photos; a silver pendant with a blue stone. It looked a little like the Bætulia Ethan had shown me, but much larger and bright blue.

Sebastian tapped on my bedroom window after dark. I opened it for him and watched him climb inside. There wasn't much room to stand, and the space between us felt steamy in the small room.

"Good thing this is a one-story house," he said, with the hint of a smirk. I wasn't in the mood for jokes. Part of me felt like I was doing something wrong, sneaking a boy into my room at night—and there was no question he got my blood pumping. But we had bigger issues. So much had happened since I'd seen him yesterday, I didn't know where to start.

"My mother was dating a Tuatha Dé," I blurted.

Sebastian raised an eyebrow and sat on my bed.

"A boy named Colin." I pulled out the photograph and showed it to him. "Ethan is his nephew. He's Tuatha Dé, too."

Sebastian's face darkened. He was angry at me.

"Going with him today was beyond stupid," he said.

"Don't worry," I said. "He doesn't know what I am. He knows about you, though. Or he thinks he does. He's never actually seen a merrow before, so he's going off old legends."

"It was reckless, and dangerous."

"Another girl was murdered yesterday, or didn't you hear? It has to stop. I couldn't just sit around and wait for another body. Someone had to do something."

"I don't know how you came to the conclusion that a rogue merrow was your responsibility," Sebastian said. He ran a casual hand through his unruly hair, which only made him more attractive. I wanted him to pin me down on the bed and kiss me brainless, but he'd made it pretty clear in the cave that we couldn't be together—at least not unless I could change fully—without breaking merrow law and endangering both of our lives. I swallowed back the longing and curled my fingers into my sweaty palms.

"Ethan's dad thinks a merrow killed Colin," I said, changing the subject. "What if it was my mother? You said there weren't many merrow around anymore. My grandmother was gone, who else could it have been?"

"Even if it's true," Sebastian said, putting his hands on my shoulders, "I'm sure it was self-defense. If Colin found out what she really was, maybe he came after her first. Maybe it was an accident."

"Or maybe my mother was a murderer," I said, feeling sick.

"It wouldn't be extraordinary. The Tuatha Dé and the merrow are at war, after all... although I don't think there have been any casualties for centuries."

"But my mom was just a girl—my age. Not a warrior."

"But like you, she had powers. She probably didn't know her own strength. It could have been a reflex, an accident. Nobody was around to show her how to control herself."

He gave me a pointed look. Is that what he thought would happen? That I'd accidently kill someone?

"What about my grandmother, Phyllis?"

"Maybe the same thing: the Tuatha Dé were always eager to find merrow blood, especially now when it's so scarce. Maybe they took Phyllis as well.

"And Father Murphy?"

"Maybe he got in the way. I don't think there's much love between the Church and the Tuatha Dé," he said, raising one eyebrow.

"Ethan may not know what you are *yet*," Sebastian continued, "but if the matching knives are any evidence, then somebody else in the Tuatha Dé already wants you dead. He'll find out soon, and spending time with him will just make him figure it out faster."

He trailed his hands down my arms and held my wrists, his fingers stroking my skin lightly. I felt an explosion of confusing emotions at his touch. *Did he know what he was doing to me?*

"I made a deal with Ethan," I admitted finally. "I told him we'd find the merrow killing the girls and deliver him to the Tuatha Dé. It was the only way to keep you safe."

"It doesn't work like that," Sebastian scowled, his eyes dark and brooding. "They'll never have enough. If they get one, they'll want ten more. Even if we deliver, they won't honor the deal: they'll kill me anyway, and then you."

"I know," I said quietly. "That's why you have to leave. It's not safe here, for you."

"Or for *you*," Sebastian said.

"Yeah, but I'm stuck here. I don't have a choice. You can transform, you can leave."

"You want me to run away and hide?" he said.

"I want you to be safe. You can't always be there to protect me. I don't want you fighting the Tuatha Dé for me, or even other merrow."

He pulled me towards him and kissed my forehead.

"That's my choice to make, not yours." My forehead was warm where his lips had pressed against it. I melted into his embrace, as he pulled me gently down onto the bed. I lay back and put my head against Sebastian's shoulder.

I hated being a burden to Sebastian. But then I remembered something else he had said earlier; that I was more powerful than I should be. Maybe I wasn't as helpless as I thought I was. Even if it was an accident, what I'd done to Roisin showed that I did have some kind of power. I just needed to learn to control it. I fell asleep with Sebastian stroking my hair, determined to discover just what I was really capable of.

25

Sebastian's brow furled as he concentrated on the still water of our private cave-pool. With his hands open, palm up, he focused on a little bit of salt water, turning it into animal shapes for me. An elephant, a giraffe, a dinosaur. They looked like little crystal figurines, sitting on top of the water.

"That's amazing," I said.

"It's a party trick. Not that useful."

Sebastian had disappeared in the middle of the night. I had to force myself to get up and go to school in the morning. Homework and tests seemed pointless, and I couldn't concentrate in class. I'd texted Sebastian to meet me at Mermaid's Cave after school. But I didn't want swimming lessons; I wanted to learn more about my abilities.

"Is that what I did to Roisin?" I asked, as a group of miniature water horses galloped across the pool.

"Yes," Sebastian said, looking uncomfortable. "But I've never heard of a mennow doing it before. Half-bloods don't usually inherit those kinds of powers. Not that I've met many half-bloods."

"Isn't there something else you could call me that's a little less insulting?"

"How about Butter-butt?" Sebastian said with a smirk, a glimmer of humor in his eyes.

I punched him in the shoulder, and skinned my knuckles against his exo, which was already as hard and rough as coral.

"Honey Bumpkin?" he said, glancing down at my body. I blushed as his eyes ran over my skin.

I thought I'd need to change fully before I had any kind of power, but maybe that wasn't true. After all, Lugh was just quarter merrow, like me, and he defeated the Fomorian army. Even if I never changed, that didn't have to mean I was helpless. I just had to figure out how it all worked.

"Why could I do it with Gatorade but not tap water?" I asked.

"Gatorade is mostly salt water," Sebastian said.

"And the Coke?"

"55mg of sodium per can. Your skin was already starting to sparkle when I pulled you away," he said.

I grimaced. *That's like drinking a pizza.*

"Your skin will react to common salt, but it's a weak substitute for actual sea water," he said.

"So how do you do it?" I said, mimicking him and placing my hands out, palm up.

"I don't know, I just, picture what I want it to do in my mind, and then reach out and connect with a little patch of water."

I tried, but I felt the enormity of the ocean. When I tried to bring it up, it felt like I was trying to move a mountain. Sweat broke out on my brow and my forearms trembled. Sebastian pushed my hands down and smiled.

"You can't move the whole ocean. Just a little bit of it. Look we don't have classes for this kind of thing, we just grow up doing it. The deeper you go, the longer you spend in the water, the more you'll understand."

"Deeper?" I asked. I'd gotten used to my own personal kiddie pool, with a few feet of crystal clear water in the gaping mouth of the cave. But the thought of going into the open ocean still terrified me.

"So what are we waiting for?" I asked, fighting down my fear. Sebastian nodded, then walked to the mouth of the cave and pulled something from the water. It looked like a cross between a jellyfish and a plastic bag.

"What's that?" I asked.

"Mer tech," he said. "It's a kind of biologically engineered breathing apparatus."

He stepped closer to me, "Don't freak out. Just keep breathing. In and out." He breathed into it, blowing it up like a balloon, then held it out towards me. I tried to stay calm as he put the thing over my head, and then squeezed it around my throat with his fingers.

"It filters the oxygen out of the water for you. With this, you can dive and breathe underwater. We use them for our young sometimes, if they are slow developers. Or for guests, long ago—though that's forbidden now."

Was this the magic cap that Galen had mentioned, that I'd read about in the legends, the *cohuleen druith*? It was kind of like wearing a big plastic helmet, and it was all fogged up.

"I can't see," I said, flailing out my arms.

"Put your head under water, try it out."

I went back into the pool and let myself sink to the bottom, like I did when I was practicing holding my breath. My face stayed completely dry. I took a small, tentative breath.

I breathed deeper, suddenly excited. It was working, and I could see everything underwater in perfect clarity. I paddled around a little, till I'd explored every corner of the cave pool. My legs kept bumping into rocks as I tried to kick around. Luckily it didn't hurt much with my toughened skin. When I came up out of the water again I had a stupid grin on my face.

"I can see everything!" I shouted.

"You don't have to yell," Sebastian said, the corners of his mouth lifting. "I'm right here."

"How do you communicate underwater?" I asked, wondering suddenly if merrow had their own language, and what it sounded like.

"It's surprisingly quiet down there, so you don't need to shout. The sound carries. But we also communicate without words. We can communicate our moods and feelings. Out of the water, those abilities are even stronger."

"I've been able to sense people's emotions recently," I said.

He nodded. "Most of us also learn human languages, and we communicate that way with each other. We tend to speak the languages that humans use where we live. I learned English and

Greek growing up. We have schools, just like you ... dry areas under the sea."

"Dry? How does that work?"

He tapped the side of my makeshift helmet.

"Picture a giant one of these. Large enough to fit an entire city inside," he said.

"It sounds beautiful," I said, my eyes shining.

"It is. Want to go see it?"

I stood up and pointed outside the cave mouth to the ocean hesitantly.

"That's right," Sebastian laughed. "Out into the open sea."

I let him take my hand and guide me out over the rocks, to the ledge of the cave, where it met the ocean. He lowered me into the water, and then climbed in beside me. It was deeper here, the water was up to my chest already, but I could still touch the bottom.

I felt the panic rising up, but I forced it back down again. I *had* to do this. Sebastian was risking his life to stay here with me. Until I could change, we were both targets.

I stuck my head under water and could see the steep drop off, leading into a dark blue void that seemed absolute and eternal. But with my enhanced vision and senses, I could feel the rifts and landscape spreading out before me. The terror was still there, but it was muted. I didn't feel as vulnerable as I had before. Maybe it was the thickened layer of merrow skin around my body, that made me feel like I was covered in superglue, or the device around my head that kept the sea from rushing in and filling my lungs. Or maybe it was having Sebastian at my side, holding on to me. I knew he wouldn't let anything bad happen.

Sebastian moved behind me and wrapped his arms around me.

"We're going for a little swim," he said. His voice sounded distant underwater, like an echo, but I could still understand him. "If at any time you feel uncomfortable, just tap on my arm and I'll take to you to the surface." I nodded.

We started off slowly, hovering just below the surface. I expected everything to be dark and cloudy in the deep waters off the coast of Northern Ireland, but with my enhanced color receptors I felt like I was on the set of Disney's *Little Mermaid*. We swam through patches of bright pink, orange, green and teal fish, and chased an enormous lobster that shot back away from us. Everything was glowing, like those black light aquariums. Then Sebastian kicked behind me with his powerful tail, and we zoomed downwards, speeding along the bottom of the ocean, leaving a cloud of sand behind us.

Sebastian pointed to the side and my eyes widened—a pod of bottle nosed dolphins were escorting us. They weaved and bobbed around us, chirping encouragement, then one by one they swam to the surface and jumped out of the water.

"Hold on," Sebastian said in my ear, pivoting and swimming upwards. We broke the surface and shot out into the sky, maybe ten feet in the air; Sebastian tucked into a somersault and I screamed as we rolled and dove back into the water again, cutting crisply. He brought me back up to the surface right after, but relaxed when he saw I was smiling.

"That was awesome." I said, out of breath. "Let's do it again."

My fears had almost disappeared. I realized that maybe it wasn't the water I'd been afraid of after all, it was the unknown. The immensity of it: being able to feel the power of the ocean, like a malevolent force, but without the ability to fight back or swim against the current. It was omnipotent, and it made me feel insignificant and worthless. It didn't care about me that day in Oregon, it didn't even know I existed, but it would have killed me all the same.

With Sebastian's arms around me, and the ability to see and breathe underwater, the overwhelming sense of terror had diminished into a slight anxiety. And at the same time, some small part of me felt an indescribable elation. It was like learning to walk or ride a bike for the first time: exhilarating *because* of the potential danger of falling down. But there was nowhere to fall down here. And the longer I spent in the water, the more confident I felt.

Sebastian pointed out a rock wall that stretched on for miles under the water, and a ring of standing stones that looked similar to the ones Ethan had shown me. It was incredible.

We took a break on a rocky island that jutted up sharply out of the water, rising to a steep, pointed peak. I was surprised to see ancient stone walls and a path leading towards the summit. He pried off the strange helmet and tucked a strand of wet hair behind my ear.

"We're about a mile away from Portrush now," Sebastian said. "This is the last bit of land before the deep water." I gulped. The water we'd just swam through had seemed plenty deep to me. Sebastian's face grew serious; nervous even. Whatever he wanted to show me next, he wasn't sure I was ready for it.

"Your mercap will help with the pressure," he said, "but you'll feel tightness in your lungs. Humans sometimes pass out at only

50 or 60 meters, which is one reason it's so easy for us to avoid them."

"How deep is the ocean?" I asked.

"On average, just over 4,000 meters." That was over two and a half miles, straight down. It would be like jumping out of an airplane. Suddenly my legs felt wobbly.

"How deep were we earlier?" I asked, trying not to let my voice waver. I was almost successful.

"About 25. Look, we don't have to go any deeper today. You've done really great so far. We could just head back."

"But you think we should keep going?" I asked.

He shrugged his shoulders. "1000 meters is as deep as the sunlight can penetrate. If we go down that deep, the pressure and darkness may force the merrow blood in you to activate."

"And then I'll change," I said hopefully.

"You *could* change. Or it might be too much for you, and you could die."

My eyes widened and my heart pounded in my chest.

"I'd never let that happen, of course," Sebastian said. "Most scuba equipment is rudimentary, so divers suffer from high blood carbon dioxide levels, or oxygen toxicity, or nitrogen narcosis. You shouldn't have any of those problems with this—" He gestured to the swimming cap I'd been wearing. "Our technology is *way* better. And your body already reacts well to the sea water, which leads me to believe you can handle the pressure. But as soon as I see any signs of you getting disoriented or passing out, I'll bring you back up."

I nodded. I trusted Sebastian. He wouldn't suggest going deeper if he really thought it was dangerous. If he was hesitating, it meant he didn't think I could handle it *emotionally*. I wanted to prove him wrong.

"What's it like down there?" I asked.

"More beautiful than you can possibly imagine," he said.

Sebastian had been laying out in the sun like a seal, but now rolled off the rocks with a splash. Colorful lights and sparkles radiated from his body in the dark water, as the ocean began the process of rebuilding his exo. I stepped in next to him, and wrapped my arms around his shoulders, preparing to let him carry me under the sea. I wasn't sure if I was ready, but it seemed riskier to just wait for someone to attack me again. If this is what it took to control my powers, so be it.

We swam around to the other side of the island, then headed out into the open sea. I gasped when I saw the ocean ledge. It was a solid wall of darkness, stretching for miles in both directions. It looked like a black void, sinking into eternity. A giant hole in the bottom of the ocean so wide and menacing I almost couldn't breathe.

Sebastian watched me, and I realized my fingers were digging into his shoulders. I tried to take the fear out of my eyes, loosening my grip and taking a few deep breaths. I bit my lip, then nodded. *Let's do this.* He kicked forward until the ground disappeared below us, and there was nothing but unfathomable darkness. A gaping, monstrous mouth, ready to swallow us whole. Then we started descending.

End of Part One

Note to the reader

Thanks for reading *Part One of Shearwater!* This is basically, just the set up to the whole story. There are a lot of little things that won't make sense until you read the complete novel. The life-shattering events in the second part of the book are what cause the characters to grow, make choices and get stronger. There are revelations about Clara, Sebastian and Ethan that will change how they see themselves, and each other. I want this to be an epic tragic romance, full of heartbreak and loss and suffering, so if it doesn't feel "deep" enough yet, I hope you'll read the complete novel when it's done. If you sign up on my newsletter, I'll not only tell you when it's ready, I'll also send you a free copy.

PS) I didn't want Clara to start off being an immediately amazing, ass-kicking heroine who was good at everything. If she seems weak or helpless so far, a damsel in distress, don't worry, she'll be a heroine you can admire by the end of the first book. But she has to go through a lot to get there. Same for Sebastian and Colin – if they seem flat still, I hope they won't when you've read the full story and gotten to know them better.

PPS) I understand publishing Part One, rather than the full novel, is really weird and might frustrate you. There are lots of reasons I decided to publish this way, but mainly it's so I can get feedback and make sure the full novel is as good as it can be. Writing is hard work and I'm learning as fast as I can. And again, this isn't just some ploy to earn more money – I'll give you the full book for free anyway if you sign up on my site.

I really hope you've enjoyed the story so far, but as a new writer I'm insecure about my craft: I would treasure a review, listing the things I've done right, and the things I've done wrong, so that I can continue to improve. Once the entire book is finished, I'll revise Part One as necessary to make it amazing, and release the full book. I hope to do that in October 2016. I'll be giving away a free trip to join me in Portballintrae, Ireland and check out all the sites in the novel, so stay tuned!

>> Sign up here to get the full book when it's ready. <<

Click here to leave a review on Amazon.

More Free Books

Shearwater is just one of a dozen novels I'm working on, with completely unique worlds and characters. If you like mermaids, vampires, angels, zombies, revolution, Faustian motifs (the dangers of technology) and post-apocalyptic or dystopian settings and scenarios, I think you'll enjoy them. I will make every book available **for free** to my followers.

>> Sign up here <<

More Mermaid Novels

Mermaids, sirens and merrow are underutilized in the world of paranormal romance, but have a lot to offer. If you love mermaids and are looking for another great book to read, I made a list of some that might interest you.

>> RECOMMENDED MERMAID BOOKS <<

Made in the USA
Lexington, KY
30 March 2017